Body Harvest
by Malcolm Rose

Published by Ransom Publishing Ltd.
Unit 7, Brocklands Farm, West Meon, Hampshire GU32 1JN, UK
www.ransom.co.uk

ISBN 978 178127 667 9
First published in 2015
Reprinted 2015

A CIP catalogue record of this book is available from the British Library.

BODY HARVEST

MALCOLM ROSE

THE OUTER REACHES

A world inhabited by two distinct and non-interbreeding humanoid species: **majors** *(the majority) and* **outers***. The two races are outwardly similar, but they have different talents, different genetics and different body chemistry.*

In this world, meet major Troy Goodhart and outer Lexi Iona Four. They form an amazing crime-fighting partnership.

SCENE 1

Monday 7th April, Early afternoon

Using a small plastic spoon, Lexi scooped up live maggots from what had once been a moist mouth. Tipping the wriggling specimens carefully into a jar of alcohol, she muttered, 'This is tricky.'

Troy turned up his nose at the dead body that had become a feast for maggots. 'It's not very nice, is it?'

Surprised, Lexi looked up at her new partner. 'I mean the opposite. Imagine how you'd feel if he was smeared all over with … What's the best food you've ever tasted?'

Troy frowned. 'Er … I don't know. Chocolate, I suppose.'

'Well, imagine he's covered in chocolate.'

'What?'

'He's making me really hungry,' Lexi said. 'Outers love maggots. Really yummy.'

Troy was a major, not an outer. He pulled a face.

Clearly in a teasing mood, Lexi added, 'At least we keep the fly population down.'

'Weird,' said Troy.

'You majors are weird to us.'

Shaking his head, Troy replied, 'Please don't eat the evidence.'

The man's corpse was lying in a shallow earthy grave which had been uncovered by a foraging fox or other woodland creature. To the side was the brushwood that someone had used to disguise the disturbed ground.

Still kneeling on the damp soil, Lexi sniffed the specimen jar and then sealed it with a sigh. 'Ah, the smell of alcohol as well.'

'Don't drink the evidence either.'

Lexi smiled. 'What did you say your name was?'

'Troy Goodhart. And you?'

'Lexi.'

'Lexi what?'

'Lexi Iona Four. I'm the fourth one.'

Troy nodded. Outers had an odd way of naming their children. As well as odd tastes in food and drink.

He looked around the clearing in the wood. Dense lines of trees shielded the spot from the quiet lane behind Troy and Langhorn Reservoir at the bottom of the slope. It was a good place to dispose of a victim. If the culprit had buried the body a little deeper, it might never have been found. Whoever had tried to cover up this particular crime must have thought that a shallow covering of earth and brushwood was enough in such an isolated place.

Lexi checked that her data logger was working and stabbed it into the ground next to the body. Every twenty minutes it would measure and record the temperature. Once it had collected the readings for a 24-hour period, she would be able to work out the time since death. Dating the development of the maggots would also help to calculate how long the body had been lying in the clearing.

Troy didn't crouch beside Lexi and the victim. He looked down at the injury to the chest, visible through the open shirt, and said, 'Do you know what killed him? Is it as obvious as it looks?'

Lexi shrugged. 'The pathologist will find out for sure. I can't tell with his clothes on and all this soil.

But ... ' She pointed to the gash directly above his heart. 'This would have finished him off, I guess.'

There was another bloodstain lower down, on his right-hand side, and possibly others. Lexi and Troy couldn't see without moving, stripping and washing the body. That wasn't their responsibility.

'No sign of a weapon,' Troy said. It was part-question, part-observation.

'I'll get a search team onto it.'

'Is he a major or an outer?' Troy asked.

Without touching the man's hands, Lexi inspected the decaying fingertips. 'Looks like an outer,' she replied. 'His DNA and the juices seeping into the soil will confirm it. I've bagged samples of decomposing fluids already.'

The stench was awful. With his superior eyesight, Troy surveyed the area as he raised the usual questions. 'Who is he?'

'No ID in his pockets,' Lexi answered. 'No mobile. They'll rummage around much more in the lab but, as far as I can see, he's got nothing on him. Not even a watch or wallet.'

'Someone's trying to stop us identifying him by taking his stuff away, or he just didn't have anything. That'd probably make him one of the displaced.'

'Maybe. Under all this earth, his clothes are pretty

manky, I think,' said Lexi. 'Straggly hair and beard as well. I'm just going to clear the rest of the maggots away so I can get a photo of his face.'

'Was he killed here?'

'Unlikely,' Lexi said. 'Not enough blood in the soil.'

'So, there's a crime scene somewhere else. And his body was probably brought here in a car – which means there'll be traces of him in it.'

'Almost certainly.'

Troy glanced back towards the road. 'You'd have to be built like a lorry to carry him from the road on your own. Maybe it was two people – or one with a wheelbarrow or something.'

'Maybe. The team'll look for footprints and tracks.'

Troy and Lexi were both wearing smooth slip-ons over their shoes so that they didn't leave any impressions on the ground.

'How long's he been here?'

'That's what the insect life will tell me, but I need more data to be accurate. These,' Lexi said, indicating the moving mass of maggots, 'are from blowflies, so he's been here more than a day. They're not very big and there aren't any pupae – you know, when the casing goes hard before the flies pop out – so it's been less than ten days.'

'Who called us in?'

'A woman who was collecting logs for her wood-burner,' Lexi replied.

'She got more than she bargained for, then. Must have been a shock.'

'Yeah.' Lexi made sure all of the samples were stored safely in her holdall and then stood up. 'I'm done. I'll let the lab people take over.' She made for the road.

'Careful,' Troy said. 'Don't trample all over the place.'

Puzzled, Lexi halted. 'What do you mean?'

'This is a perfect place for getting rid of bodies, isn't it?'

The large, rectangular clearing consisted of bare soil near to the trees, but grass and wild flowers had taken over the centre. It was early April, sunnier than normal, and bluebells were beginning to colour the edges of the space while white and yellow petals flecked the middle.

'I suppose.'

'Look,' Troy said, pointing towards two patches of turf that were a slightly lighter colour than the rest, with fewer wild flowers.

'Younger growth,' Lexi suggested.

'Why are they like that?'

Lexi shrugged again.

'You call in the lab guys,' Troy said, clutching his life-logger. 'I'm going to ask for ground-penetrating radar. And sniffer dogs.'

Lexi stared at him, surprised at his attention to detail. 'You think someone's been digging more graves.'

'Just a feeling.'

Carefully, they picked their way back up the slope to the rarely used lane. The two young detectives were the same age as each other and the same height. They were both fit and somewhat shorter than average. Lexi looked wiry and fast. Troy was sturdier, probably slower, but more powerful. Without a close look, it was difficult to tell which one of them was the major and which was the outer. Externally, the two human species were similar. Internally, though, the body chemistry of a major was very different from that of an outer.

Troy had bright red hair. On his cheeks and chin were the first signs of ginger stubble. A faint moustache was making its appearance above his lip. His bright eyes – a penetrating blue – suggested that he had great powers of observation.

Lexi's hair was cut short, revealing an attractive face with a steely expression of determination. She wore no make-up on her bronzed skin. Her striking hair colour – somewhere between blonde and silver – made her look older than her sixteen years. Like any outer, her fingertips were smooth and did not leave prints on anything she touched.

'Is this your first case?' she asked Troy.

'Is it that obvious?'

A faint smile was her reply.

Troy gazed at her and said, 'What happened to your last partner?'

'We didn't get on.'

'Oh. What's wrong with you?' He grinned to show that he was joking.

'Nothing. It was her. To be honest, I didn't think she was ... clever enough.'

'All outers say they're north of majors when it comes to cleverness.'

'That's because we are. No doubt about it. It's been measured scientifically. But this particular major held me back.'

Troy admitted, 'I'm not clever either. Not really.'

'What are you, then? You must have something special to become a detective.'

'My reports always said I was perceptive. I didn't know what it meant at first. I had to look it up.'

Lexi nodded. 'That'll do. I can work with perceptive. Me, I was always called methodical.'

'Sounds boring.'

'I like following procedures,' she replied. 'It gets results.'

'Do you *always* get results?'

'With the right partner, yes.'

Emerging from the last line of trees and ducking under the police tape, they stopped beside the road and removed their slip-ons. Troy turned towards Lexi and said, 'I don't think I'll hold you back.'

She looked him up and down. 'We'll see.'

There were two uniformed officers on duty, guarding the crime scene. 'We've finished for now,' Lexi told them. 'There are teams on their way, though. More tests and searches, and a body to take to the pathologist. Maybe more digging as well. We don't have to be here while they do it but you're stuck, I'm afraid.'

'Hope you've got toothbrushes and a change of clothes,' Troy added. 'We'll be back if anything else turns up.'

Every detective carried a life-logger. Lexi and Troy each had one of the small mobile devices and it stored every aspect of their working lives. It recorded everything they did, everywhere they went, and everything they saw, heard and said. It provided the evidence in any later trial and ensured that the investigation had been conducted correctly. Lexi's and Troy's life-loggers had already sent their requirements to the coming teams.

The two teenage detectives had come separately to the crime scene, but they were leaving together. Lexi secured her precious holdall in the boot of the police car and then they both got in. Talking to the onboard computer, Lexi said, 'Shepford Crime Central.' As the car accelerated, they knew that they were about to spend a lot of time in each other's company. If they worked well together, they would form a partnership and tackle many more cases.

SCENE 2

Monday 7th April, Afternoon

Analysing the fluid leaking from the corpse first, Lexi was looking at the peaks and troughs on the chromatogram. 'I don't need to wait for the DNA result,' she announced. 'This is the normal profile of decay products from an outer.' She tapped out a few instructions on the keypad and added, 'The computer says it's a ninety-seven per cent match.'

On the other side of the large glass panel, forensic scientists were working on several different cases in a totally clean environment. One of them was measuring the maggots that Lexi had plucked from the body. Two were staring at paint flakes and fibres through microscopes. Others were preparing samples for various chemical analysers. Some were comparing fingerprints or examining handwriting. Each of them was dressed in an all-over white lab coat. Troy and Lexi were sitting in the attached computer room.

'A bit depressing really,' Troy said.

'What is?'

'One day, we all decompose to smelly goo and seep into the ground.'

'That's nature for you,' Lexi said cheerfully. 'It's beautiful. But don't you believe there's a mysterious spirit that leaves the body before rot sets in? The essence of major's gone before nature starts to recycle the body.'

Troy nodded. 'There's got to be more than feeding flies and bacteria.'

'Has there?' Lexi said with a twisted smile. 'I don't know why. There's life and there's death. I've never seen anything in-between. No sign of life after death. And no body scanner's ever found a soul – or whatever you want to call it.'

Troy took a swig of blueberry juice and said, 'I don't think we're going to settle this right now.'

'You're scared of losing the argument.'

'I've just got other things on my mind,' Troy replied.

'Like a murder.' Knowing that Lexi's life-logger would have many images of the victim, he asked, 'Have you uploaded a picture of him?'

She nodded. 'I had to clean up the ones of his face for ID purposes. The computer still doesn't recognize him. And he doesn't match anyone on the missing persons' list either. We're going to have to work harder to find out who he is.'

Lexi's drink was different. It was mulled wine and Troy could smell the warm alcoholic vapour. Outers drank beer, wine and cider from an early age because alcohol nourished them like any other food. Unlike majors, their bodies lacked the metabolic pathway that caused intoxication, so alcohol didn't damage their organs and they never got drunk.

'Maybe his DNA will be in the database,' Troy said before hesitating and adding, 'Or is that too easy as well?'

'We'll find out tomorrow.'

Troy typed a few commands on the keypad until the screen showed him a satellite image of the area where the body had been found. He cocked his head on one side and murmured, 'Why here?'

Lexi shrugged. 'Because it's remote? Not many people go there.'

'Our bad guy knows all about it, though.'

'Maybe he collects logs as well.'

'So he'd have a wood-burning stove.'

'Or he's into wood-carving,' Lexi replied with a smirk.

'My point exactly,' said Troy. 'Place always tells a story. In this case, we just don't know what it is yet.' Examining the map again, he said, 'Could be a lot of deer roaming around, so maybe he's into hunting. Maybe he – or *she* – goes sailing on the reservoir. Maybe he's a tree surgeon. I don't know, but there'll be a connection for sure.'

'We'll probably pin it down after forensics have solved the case.'

Troy frowned and turned back to the monitor. He zoomed out to get an overall view of the area. 'I'll run a check on every building within ten kilometres.'

Lexi peered at the map. 'Won't take long. Probably a few farms, a yachting club and the waterworks. That's the lot, isn't it?'

'Maybe one of the farmers is a mad, tree-felling, wood-carving murderer.'

Lexi laughed. 'No chance. Anyone like that would use an axe or a chainsaw. Ours is nowhere near as messy.'

All murder detectives laughed a lot. Troy knew why. It was the way they protected themselves from the awful things they saw. They had to cleanse themselves of the violence committed by both human races and they did it with dark humour. If they didn't laugh, they'd probably cry.

'What are those maggots telling you?'

'At this time of year, flies would have found the body within an hour and laid eggs on the moist bits – the mouth, eyes, armpits and open wounds. The maggots would have hatched in twelve to twenty-four hours and started munching straightaway. The ones I sampled were under a centimetre long. That's two days' growth or thereabouts, but it depends a lot on temperature. I'm still waiting for those readings.'

Troy looked down at his life-logger. 'They want us back at the field,' he announced.

Lexi nodded and stood up. 'That means you were right. More bodies.'

SCENE 3

Monday 7th April, Early evening

The wood was no longer empty and peaceful. It was heaving with crime scene officers in white overalls. To Troy's left, a line of policemen and women on their hands and knees stretched across the clearing. They were inching forward slowly, conducting a fingertip search for a weapon – or anything else that might be relevant. Two officers were coming to the end of their zigzag inspection of the area with ground-penetrating radar. Forensic scientists were carrying sealed bags back to the vehicles parked in the narrow lane beyond the trees. The team had found two more bodies, exactly where Troy had predicted. A small digger was parked between two new holes and four small mounds of soil. The pathologist – an outer called Kofi Seven – had removed the body that Lexi and Troy had already seen. Now he was examining another in a makeshift grave.

Walking beside Troy, Lexi said, 'If there was a god, he'd have put a stop to stuff like this.'

'It doesn't work like that,' Troy retorted. 'Majors and outers have free will.'

'Huh.'

They stopped and looked down into the first freshly dug hollow. This time, it was a woman. The corpse was too dirty and rotten to reveal much.

Kofi shook his head. 'Don't ask. I've got to get this one back to the lab before I can tell you anything. No obvious wounds, though.'

'What about … ?' Troy waved his arm towards the second hole.

'A male in an advanced state of decay, missing his right hand.'

Troy walked to the hollow, glanced down and shuddered. From head to stomach, the man was soiled but apparently whole. Below his waist, he was incredibly thin, as if the bottom part of his body had rotted much quicker than the top. Troy looked away.

'The body's very fragile,' the pathologist said. 'I'm still figuring out how to take it away in one piece.'

'Cause of death?' Lexi asked.

'To be decided, but his throat's been slit.'

Troy flinched but kept his distaste to himself. Lexi did not react.

'Come and see me in the morning,' Kofi said. 'I'll have a good picture by then.'

Signalling to the crime scene supervisor, Lexi asked, 'Have you found a weapon?'

She shook her head. 'No.'

'That fits – if the killing was done somewhere else,' Troy said.

The supervisor told them, 'We've bagged a lot of stuff, but I'm not sure we've got anything worthwhile.'

'Tyre impressions or footprints?'

'Possible faint trolley or cart tracks. It's hard to say. But maybe that's how the bodies got here. At least three sets of shoeprints so far. One probably belongs to the woman who found the first body.'

Lexi nodded. 'Keep looking.'

SCENE 4

Tuesday 8th April, Morning

The bright white pathology laboratory was not Troy's favourite place. Laid out on plinths, human bodies were objects for undignified exploration. To Troy, pathologists resembled customs officers who opened up suspicious suitcases and delved inside, putting aside clothes and possessions to uncover hidden evidence. They went to great lengths to discover the causes of death, apparently able to detach themselves from a person whose internal organs they lifted out, whose brain they accessed with a saw.

Kofi was tall and lean with a shaved head and

large blue trainers. His feet had to be enormous. He towered over the three bodies that he'd labelled L4G#1, L4G#2 and L4G#3. L4G stood for Lexi Four/Goodhart. He would not understand Troy's distress that, in the absence of real names, the victims had been given heartless codes.

'You'll recognize L4G#1,' Kofi said. 'A male outer, about thirty years of age. No ID of any sort.'

Lexi nodded. The result of the DNA test that she'd requested yesterday had come in. The victim was definitely an outer, but his profile was not in the DNA database so his identity remained a mystery.

Kofi glanced at Lexi and said, 'With all this hair he's got, I'm not surprised you missed a blow to the back of the head with a heavy, blunt object.'

Lexi asked, 'Was it lethal?'

'No. It would just have knocked him out.'

'So, what killed him?' said Troy

'Prepare yourselves.'

'What?' Troy prompted.

'He has no heart, liver or kidneys.'

'How do you mean?'

'Cause of death: removal of heart, liver and kidneys. That's why he's lying here. It's hard to regain consciousness without a heart.'

'That's ... ' Troy was lost for words.

'Unusual?' Kofi suggested. 'And rather intriguing.'

Finding his voice again, Troy asked, 'Was it done … professionally? Can you tell?'

'It wasn't someone hacking away in a frenzied attack. It was done with a very sharp knife or a scalpel – and with care. But, no, it wasn't up to operating theatre standard. And no one bothered to sew up the wounds afterwards.'

Lexi seemed to be suppressing anger. 'What's your estimate for when he died?'

'He's cold and rigor mortis has come and gone.' He lifted the left arm by the wrist and the hand flopped. 'Totally flaccid. That tells me he died more than thirty-six hours ago. The entomologist says there were no beetles, mites, ants or wasps, so he's fairly fresh. Two or three days. You'll be able to pin it down yourself, won't you?'

Lexi nodded again. 'I'm collecting temperature evidence right now. As long as the weather doesn't change … Hey presto.'

Knowing that Kofi will have examined the man's stomach contents during the post-mortem, she asked, 'What was his last meal?'

'Bug burger and chips. Mostly locusts.'

Troy turned up his nose.

'Huh. You eat cow, don't you?' Lexi snapped at him.

'Beef, yes,' Troy replied.

'Well, insects and arachnids are twelve times more efficient than cows at turning plants into edible protein. And they taste better.'

Kofi smiled at their bickering. 'Do either of you want to hear about your second corpse? She's fascinating as well. Maybe more so.'

'Yes.'

Kofi turned towards the plump body that had a tag dangling from the left big toe. It labelled her as L4G#2. 'She's a major but an overnight DNA test tells me she's got an outer heart.'

'What?' Troy exclaimed. 'How's that possible?'

Major and outer body parts looked much the same but their chemistry was different. They were completely incompatible.

'Surgery. A bizarre – and very cruel – experiment or a transplant that went wrong because of an organ mix-up.'

Troy and Lexi exchanged a glance. Last night, when Troy had researched all of the buildings near the clearing, he'd found a reference to the Rural Retreat Transplant Clinic, situated at the far end of the reservoir.

Lexi asked, 'How long would she survive with the wrong heart?'

'A few hours at most. Her immune system would have rejected it pretty quickly.'

'I don't suppose it's the first body's heart, is it?' Troy asked.

'No. You can't link them like that, I'm afraid. She died maybe a week before him.' Kofi hesitated and then said, 'Of course, despite appearances, it means you've really got four victims. The only thing we've got of L4G#4 is a heart. The DNA doesn't match any database, so all we know is that he or she's an outer.'

'Here's something easier. Have you identified her – L4G#2?' Lexi asked.

'No,' Kofi answered. 'But it's interesting that there's an illegal trade in body parts. Do you know? There's a lot of money to be made, trading organs like hearts and lungs. The displaced and bodies stolen from mortuaries are prime sources. Look at L4G#1. Unshaven and unkempt, missing some valuable organs. There's a possible connection. Which brings me nicely to L4G#3. He's not one of the displaced, but he's your most extreme victim.'

'What do you mean?'

'He's a major and he's missing a heart, lungs, eyes,

liver and kidneys. On top of that … ' Theatrically, he waved an arm over the lower part of the body. From the withered stomach, L4G#3 was nearly flat. 'Almost all the bones below his waist have been harvested. That's why he's two-dimensional down there.'

'You mean,' Troy struggled to say, 'someone's taken his bones out? Why … ?'

'Bones are useful for making dental implants. He's been fairly thoroughly ransacked for anything useful. Note the missing right hand. And there's no skin on his back. I imagine that went to a burns victim.'

'But all this … surgery would have been done after he died, wouldn't it?' Troy said. 'I hope so.'

Kofi nodded. 'The police were wrong about the cause of death.'

Troy was puzzled. 'The police know about him?'

'Yes. We've identified him … '

Troy interrupted. 'Let's drop the code, then. Show him some respect and use his name.'

Taken aback by Troy's vehemence, Kofi replied, 'Er … Sure. He's Dmitri Backhouse – thirty-eight years old – and he went missing six weeks ago, presumed suicide … '

'Suicide?' Lexi exclaimed.

'According to his medical notes, he'd tried twice before and failed. He'd visited lots of suicide chat rooms. The police assumed he'd succeeded on the third attempt.'

'But ... '

With a grin, Kofi said, 'I know. He's the first suicide I've come across who's slit his own throat – that's how he died – and afterwards removed various body parts before burying himself.'

'So,' Troy replied, 'we're talking assisted suicide or something more ... '

'Murderous?' Lexi offered.

'Assisted suicide's murder. No, I meant, a more ordinary killing.'

'I'll upload everything for you,' Kofi told them. 'You know, I envy you two, in a way.'

'How come?' Lexi asked.

'It's a remarkable case. You're lucky to get it.'

'We'll see,' Lexi muttered.

On the way out, Troy asked Kofi, 'Have you ever had any bodies stolen from here? I'm thinking about stuff being bought and sold for transplants. Have you got first-hand experience?'

The pathologist shook his head. 'I know about it, but I'm not part of it.'

SCENE 5

Tuesday 8th April, Midday

As the driverless car approached the area where Dmitri Backhouse and the other two victims had been abandoned, Troy glanced across at Lexi. 'Are you asleep?' he asked.

'No,' she said, slowly opening her eyes. 'I'm meditating. At least, I was.'

Troy knew perfectly well that outers did not sleep. Instead, they switched off for short regular periods. Teasing her, he said, 'Meditating? That's just a fancy word for thinking, isn't it?'

'No. It's the opposite of thinking – and much deeper.

It's a sort of mental drifting. A way of de-stressing. It stops impulsive reactions to emotional events – like crime. Afterwards, thoughts are much clearer. Much sharper.' She looked at Troy and added, 'You know what everyone does when their computer goes wrong?'

'Turn it off and back on again?'

'That's what outers do up here.' She tapped the side of her head. 'When our brains get cluttered, we turn them off and turn them back on again fifteen minutes later. Hey presto. Works every time – unless we're interrupted.'

'Well, we're arriving. You'd have to snap out of it anyway.'

They left the car and walked first to the home of the witness who'd reported seeing the body they now called L4G#1. Her small rustic cottage lay near to the water treatment office, but out of its sight.

The woman who answered the knocker was in her fifties and she appeared to be in good health. Surprised that she should have visitors, she looked at the two young detectives and muttered, 'Yes?'

Troy introduced himself and his partner. 'We just wanted to ask you a few questions about your recent … find in the wood.'

Reluctantly, she stood to one side. Sighing, she said, 'Come in.'

The living room was at the rear of the property and there were no trees to obscure the view over Langhorn Reservoir. Curiously old-fashioned, there was a large black wood-burner in one corner and a bulky television in another. Some ancient music was playing on an out-dated music system that Troy and Lexi hardly recognized. Modern technology had passed by Avril Smallcross.

She turned off the music and ushered them towards a sofa. 'Sit,' she said, almost as if talking to a pet dog.

Lexi remained on her feet but Troy perched on the edge of the leather couch. 'Do you live here on your own?' he asked.

'Yes.'

'It must be lonely.'

'The young and the old want different things out of life. Maybe you like the buzz of a city. I prefer peace and quiet.'

'Do you work?'

'Retired.'

Troy nodded. 'You were out collecting wood.'

'I walk a lot,' Avril told him. 'Keeps me fit. It's a waste not to pick up wood for the stove while I'm at it.'

'Have you ever seen people digging in the clearing?'

She frowned. 'Not that I recall.'

Lexi said, 'Did you go up close to the body?'

'No. But close enough, thank you. What happened to the poor man?'

Troy didn't want to go into details. 'We're still looking into it,' he replied. 'Did you recognize him? Have you seen him round here before?'

'I didn't exactly study him, but ... ' Avril shook her head.

'Have you ever worked in health or got involved in medical operations?'

'No. What a strange question. Why?'

'We were wondering if you've had anything to do with transplants.'

'Oh, I see. You're thinking of the clinic down the road. No. Never been there. Is it relevant?'

Troy shrugged. 'Probably not.' In truth, the Rural Retreat Transplant Clinic was his main priority for the day.

'You wouldn't know by looking at me now,' she said, 'but I used to be a lifeboat pilot.'

'Exciting,' Lexi replied. 'I always fancied being a pilot. Of anything fast. Anyway, have you got the shoes you were wearing when you found the body?'

'Er ... That'd be my walking boots. Yes.'

'I need to take a photo of the tread.'

'Why?'

'There were shoeprints in the clearing. I need to eliminate yours,' Lexi explained. 'The rest might belong to whoever dumped the body.'

'I see. Wait. I'll get them.'

By the time they left Avril's cottage, Lexi had several images of the soles of Avril's walking boots on her life-logger and Troy had his thoughts about the woman who had stumbled across the primitive burial ground.

Together, Troy and Lexi retraced Avril's route to the crime scene. There, Lexi retrieved her data logger, complete with its precious information on temperature. Encircled by police ribbon, the clearing was still guarded by officers and the search team was nearing the end of its hunt for a weapon and other clues.

The two detectives had decided to make for the transplant clinic on foot because a long waterside stroll would give them a better picture of the area.

While they walked, Troy said, 'You looked … annoyed in the mortuary.'

'Did I?'

'Like someone or something was niggling you.'

'Yes, well, I don't like the idea of someone defiling bodies by removing this and that.'

'You're not squeamish or religious.'

'You don't have to be to know it's wrong. It's like slashing a great work of art.' She paused before adding, 'To me, our insides are just as beautiful as our outsides.'

Troy grimaced. 'You get to see enough of them in this job.'

Sarcastically, Lexi replied, 'I'm lucky like that.'

The rough path was almost straight, keeping parallel to the reservoir. At the water's edge, there were a few wooden platforms for fishing but they were all rickety and vacant. The trees were mostly firs. Under a high green roof, the wood was bare and dark, even sinister. Tapering as it approached the end of the reservoir, it was also eerily quiet.

'Transplants are different for outers, aren't they?' Troy said.

'We don't go in for different blood groups like you majors, if that's what you mean. For us, it's one type fits all. No need to match the donor and recipient. Any outer heart, liver or whatever will be okay for any other outer. Convenient.'

Abruptly, she halted.

Troy looked back at her and whispered, 'What is it?'

'There's someone over there,' Lexi said, pointing away from the water's edge.

She was right. Troy could just make out a small log cabin, topped with a roof of bundled twigs. Outside it, a man was sitting at a crooked table, examining a piece of wood.

Lexi and Troy looked at each other. 'Well?' Lexi said. 'Are we walkers who just happened to come this way or are we detectives? Official or unofficial?'

Troy knew it was his call. Lexi took care of the forensic side of the investigation. His strength was in dealing with people and questioning. He felt forced to make a quick decision because he knew Lexi did not like to be held back. 'Er ... Official but friendly. And curious.'

Lexi nodded.

Together they left the track and ambled towards the man and his shack. He wasn't old. Perhaps nearing thirty. He was rough rather than dirty. He had long black hair but no beard. 'Hi,' Troy called out, noting the woodworking tools scattered around the table. A large axe and a fishing rod were propped against the side of the cabin.

The man smiled, showing startlingly white teeth. 'Nice morning.'

'I'm Troy. This is Lexi. For some reason, the powers-that-be made us detectives.'

'Thought so,' he said, putting down the piece of wood. 'I'm not doing anything against the law.'

'No problem. Do you live here?'

'Yep,' he answered, as if he didn't have a care in the world. Wearing shorts and a T-shirt, he didn't seem to feel the chill breeze.

'You're one of the displaced.'

'Never did like that label but ... ' He shrugged.

'Was it your choice?' Troy asked.

'They called me a maths genius, but I opted out. Yes, my choice. It's a good life.'

'What's your name?'

'Huw.'

Troy didn't push for a surname. He wanted to keep it informal. 'Not exactly state-of-the-art living.'

Huw laughed. 'Everyone owns too much stuff. You don't need it. I've got shelter, a bed, clothes, wood to keep me warm in winter, plenty of food ... '

Troy interrupted. 'Where from?'

'I grow it, catch it or just pick it up. Fish, squirrels, road-kill, vegetables. Lots. A hole in the ground's my toilet. For water, I filter rain through sand. Easy.'

Troy grimaced. 'You drink it?'

'I filter it through sand *and* charcoal to make it drinkable.' He waved a hand over his traditional tools. 'Carving gives me trinkets to sell if I need money for something nature doesn't provide for free.'

Troy wondered if he'd found that mad, tree-felling, wood-carving murderer, but Huw came across as harmless. Even so, Lexi must have been thinking the same because she was examining the sharp tools lined up on the table, almost certainly checking for bloodstains.

'What about company?'

'It's not necessary,' Huw answered. 'But I can go into the city if the mood takes me. Before I came here, I worked as a volunteer at a homeless centre. It was good. I might do it again if I move on.'

'Do you ever see anyone around here?' Troy asked.

'Sometimes. Not a lot.'

'A woman called Avril Smallcross who lives up there?' Troy said, pointing in the general direction. 'She walks, collects wood.'

'I've seen her.'

'Anyone else? Any visitors in the last few days or weeks?'

'No one I took notice of.'

'Have you seen anything weird going on between here and Avril's house?'

'This is sounding like an interrogation.'

'Do you know what happened in the clearing back there?'

Huw shook his head. 'Nothing to do with me.'

Troy turned to look the other way. 'What do you know about the transplant clinic?'

'Zero.' He thumped his chest cheerfully. 'I'll make do with the heart that's got me this far. It didn't cost anything, either.'

Troy smiled. 'Are you staying put? Not planning to move?'

'I'll still be here if you come back with some more questions,' Huw replied. 'But I don't know how I can help – unless you decide to break loose. Give up crime and I could show you how to live the good life.'

Lexi and Troy continued their walk. In another twenty-five minutes, they arrived at the Rural Retreat Transplant Clinic. Contrasting with Huw's basic home, the private surgery was a large modern building with lots of gentle curves and glass. Outside was an attractive water feature with an impressive fountain. Troy guessed that it was supposed to be soothing. Inside, the floor was bare wood and the pastel walls were decorated with paintings and prints. The atmosphere was sheer luxury.

Troy and Lexi were ushered into a roomy office

belonging to the manager of the clinic. Behind an enormous desk, Gianna Humble stood up, walked round and greeted them. She sat in a comfy chair and waved them towards two leather seats. Clearly, she didn't allow a desk to come between her and her clients. 'You're welcome,' she said with a bright smile, 'but … What can I do for you?'

Troy told her that they were investigating three deaths but didn't mention the nearby burial site. He skipped the details, giving just enough information to suggest a link to medical transplants. 'So,' he said, 'I hope you can help us in a few ways. Like, we want to know if one of the victims was a patient of yours and where your body parts come from.'

Gianna cut him short. 'Let's take it a step at a time. Our main business here is hearts, lungs, liver and kidneys, but we've also branched out into hands and faces … '

'Faces?'

She nodded. 'For those with facial tumours, or who've been disfigured by fire or animal attack.'

'Where do you get them from? Not just faces. Everything.'

'I couldn't possibly discuss individual donors – the source of the tissue we use. I have to protect their anonymity. Besides, talking about this heart or that hand is tactless. The bereaved family and friends wouldn't thank me for giving the impression that the remains of their loved ones are merely spare parts – or health products.'

'Are they legal, though?'

'Of course,' Gianna replied. 'But I'm afraid you're right to imply there's an illegal market. We would never have anything to do with it, though.'

Troy felt as if he was under some sort of test and his new partner was the silent examiner. He imagined Lexi assessing his verbal tussle with this slick and clever manager. 'Is it ... you know ... quite common? Does it happen a lot?'

'Desperate people will part with considerable sums of money so, yes, it's out there. You see, the human body provides a rich and long harvest.'

'What do you mean?' Troy asked.

'Think of what it offers and when. There are useful parts from before birth until after death. From female eggs – especially majors' eggs – through to skin, hearts and kidneys as soon as the old owner no longer needs them. Some are more valuable than others. Of the common transplants, a lung costs the most. Then it's heart, liver, kidney, cornea, and eggs in that order. On top of that, genetics enters into the reckoning. If a woman's young and healthy, tall, good-looking, athletic and musical, she'll get a higher price for selling her eggs because that's what the clients value most.'

'You know a lot about it.'

Gianna's eyes narrowed for a moment. 'It's my job to know – without getting personally involved in the illicit trade. You're welcome to look around anywhere you like – apart from sterile treatment areas, of course – and check our records if you wish, with the exception of confidential files.'

On the surface, Gianna Humble gave the impression of being helpful and open, but Troy realized that she would reveal only a little. He guessed that the confidential files were the ones he most wanted to see. 'We'd like a tour, for sure – and as much information on your clients and sources as you can give us – but first ... These people whose body parts get harvested illegally. Who are they? Where do they come from?'

'Mortuaries mainly, I believe,' she answered. 'Rumour has it that certain overseas prisoners are executed for their organs as well.'

'What about people who've killed themselves?'

'I'm not aware of that. But ... '

'Yes?'

'It makes a perverted sort of sense. If someone

were helping people to commit suicide, they could make sure the method doesn't damage the valuable organs and then remove them quickly. After all, the deceased don't need them.'

Troy said, 'People thinking about killing themselves aren't in it for money.' Thinking aloud, he added, 'I suppose their friends and family might be, though. Someone could assist a suicide, take the valuable bits, pay the relatives or whoever, and then sell the organs on the black market.'

Gianna shrugged. 'Sounds feasible, but it's all guesswork.' She got to her feet, saying, 'I'll show you around.'

While she escorted them along clean, quiet and classy corridors, Troy asked, 'Why are you here? I mean, tucked away in the middle of nowhere.'

'Our clients recover much quicker in a relaxed atmosphere. They appreciate tranquillity.'

It was certainly peaceful. No one was rushing around with patients on trolleys. Two nurses walked from one room to another, talking quietly to each other. At the far end of one passageway, a man was mopping the floor almost noiselessly. There were no alarms or sirens, no traffic noise, no obvious emergencies. Faint regular bleeping noises sounded from some of the side-rooms. Everywhere was the reassuring whiff of disinfectant.

'Have you transplanted a right hand recently?'

'No. A left, yes, but not a right.'

Gianna took them into a reception area at the back of the building. 'This,' she announced, 'is where all our tissue arrives. Out of a specialised delivery van, straight through that hatch and into here where the barcodes and details are double-checked.'

Troy and Lexi looked around. It was a simple room containing a large chiller, two computer terminals, various medical tools and small pieces of equipment. 'So,' Troy said, 'you don't get whole bodies.'

'No. The organs arrive – usually from hospitals – in sealed sterilized containers. Each is barcoded at source.'

'Have you ever heard of a major getting an outer body part by accident?'

She laughed dismissively. 'It can't happen. We have strict procedures. From here they go to a sterile area for visual and analytical checks. Some are used as soon as the tests are complete. Some are chilled until the recipient is prepared.'

'But could a mix-up happen? Somewhere else?'

'Not in any hospital adhering to the right and proper guidelines. If there was a rogue clinic – an underground one – I suppose the standards wouldn't be so rigorous.'

'Do you know any illegal places?'

'No,' she answered tersely.

'Where's your nearest competition?'

On her way out of the room, she replied, 'I don't regard other clinics as competition. And I like to think we're unique around here.'

Following her, Lexi said, 'You must have very experienced doctors.'

'We used to have two house surgeons. Ely Eight and – appropriately enough – Blade Five, but we lost Ely to retirement. When necessary, Blade brings in specialists to assist with particular transplants. But, yes, he's highly skilled.'

Troy knew by instinct that Lexi was wondering who was capable of removing the heart, liver and kidneys of L4G#1 with a sharp knife or scalpel. He hung back by the window for a moment, watching a smartly dressed and broad-shouldered man walking away from the clinic's rear exit. His baseball cap seemed out of place.

'Come,' the manager said. 'I'll show you all our records – at least the ones without patients' confidential details.'

'We could force you to hand everything over,' Troy told her.

'To get a warrant,' she replied, 'you'd have to have

good evidence we'd done something wrong.' She spread her arms. 'There's no such evidence – because we haven't.'

SCENE 6

Tuesday 8th April, Evening

They'd visited the water treatment office, the yachting club and every farm in the area and learned nothing more. Tired and hungry, they'd wolfed down their main courses and were finishing off their meal with puddings. Troy tucked into ice cream and Lexi had a plateful of chocolate-dipped candied ginger crickets.

Troy swallowed a mango-flavoured mouthful. 'Maybe the Rural Retreat's got a hidden basement for illicit transplants.'

'Or – what did Kofi say? – bizarre medical

experiments.' Lexi glanced down at her vibrating life-logger and read the incoming message. 'The weapon search didn't turn anything up.'

Troy groaned, because any investigation was a lot easier when forensics had the murder weapon. 'At least you've got the measurements you need to pin down when the latest body was left in the wood, haven't you?'

'Yes. And the footprint data.'

'The last meal he had,' said Troy. 'Locust burger. Is that common?'

'As common as ... chips. Which he also had. So you can't trace him through a restaurant or kitchen where he got it.' Tapping her life-logger, Lexi said, 'I'm requesting a list of all known patients who've had a hand transplant.'

'That fits. I'd really like to talk to whoever's got Dmitri Backhouse's,' Troy replied. 'And if someone helped him to die ... I'll check out suicide chat rooms.'

Grinning, Lexi said, 'That'll be a right good laugh.'

Troy grunted. Changing the subject, he asked her, 'Do you speak outer?'

'Not very well. English got forced on us at school. Rotten language.'

'Is it?'

'What are you eating?'

Troy looked down. 'Ice cream.'

'Yes. It's a stupid language when you can't tell the difference between your pudding and "I scream".' She mimicked a silent scream. 'Then there's "I sing" and the stuff on a cake.'

Troy nodded and smiled. 'I see what you mean.'

'It's even tricky to tell the difference between "new displays" and "nudist plays".'

Troy laughed. 'I've never been to a nudist play. Sounds revolting.'

After the meal, Lexi settled into a chair and calmly closed her eyes. She took five deep breaths and relaxed into meditation.

With a sigh, Troy turned on his computer and went online. He knew he'd have fifteen uninterrupted minutes.

According to the police files on Dmitri Backhouse, he'd visited a suicide chat room under a username of Backdown. Troy scrolled through endless entries, reading Backdown's gloomy contributions and looking for any other user who'd encouraged him to die.

There was nothing obvious. Some contributors discussed methods of dying, mostly focusing on degree of pain and certainty of success. Some visitors were endlessly optimistic, probably part of a caring charity, pleading with visitors to seek help. Others were supportive of the decision to end life, but they stopped short of promoting it.

It was clear from his postings that Dmitri Backhouse had lost his faith in God. Like an outer, he saw nothing but the laws of nature. And that had destroyed his sense of worth.

'If there's nothing after death, why am I bothering to live? What's the point? Eighty pointless years. I don't get it.'

Three visitors had responded almost immediately.

'Take heart. Outers have no faith. They still lead fulfilling lives.'

'No road goes on for ever, but they all pass through interesting places before they come to an end.'

'The point is to help others. There are many ways of doing it. Some are surprising.'

It was the third message that grabbed Troy's attention. Was it referring to donating organs after death? It had been posted by someone with a username of Charon Angel.

That triggered something in Troy's memory. He'd heard of Charon. Two minutes of online research told him that, in mythology, Charon was the ferryman who carried the souls of the dead across the River Styx to the underworld. He was the guide between the land of the living and the land of the dead. And he always required payment.

Troy was still staring at the information on the legend when Lexi stirred. Looking up, he said, 'All systems back up and running?'

'Mmm. How's it going?'

Troy shook his head grimly. 'This job really depresses me.'

Lexi looked surprised. 'Does it? But you've hardly … ' She stopped when she saw Troy break into a mischievous smile.

'Razor-sharp mind after you've turned it back on again, eh?' he said.

Lexi nodded. 'You're going to play a suicidal role online. You want our bad guy to notice your postings and get in touch – if he exists.'

'Exactly,' Troy replied. '*I'm a waste of space. Someone else could do so much more than me*. At least, that's the sort of thing I'm going to write. My body's the bait.'

'Good idea. Dangerous tactic.'

'I don't mind a bumpy ride – as long as it works.'

Lexi turned towards her own terminal. Her forensic software soon identified the tread of Avril Smallcross's walking boots among the three sets of impressions near the burial site. The computer defined Unknown Shoeprint 1 as trainer-type, 29.6 cm length (size 12), manufactured by Adibok, no significant wear on either tread. Unknown Shoeprint 2 was smaller: standard walking shoe / boot, 26.2 cm length (size 8), unknown manufacturer, both heels worn, chipped rubber in centre of left shoe.

Putting the graph of round-the-clock temperatures on screen, Lexi assumed that the conditions hadn't changed much in the last few days. She added into the equation the extent of maggot development and L4G#1's body temperature when she measured it yesterday. And she calculated that L4G#1 had died on Friday evening and been dumped in the wood very shortly afterwards.

'It's warmer than average for April,' she said. 'The maggots have lapped it up. I'm pretty sure all the action was on Friday night.'

'Someone used the cover of darkness to dump the body, then.'

'More than likely.'

SCENE 7

Tuesday 8th April, Night

The experimental music wafted around the room where Lexi relaxed with friends. An outer boy said with a grin, 'So, you've got a new partner in crime. A major. Watch your back is all I'm saying.'

Lexi smiled. 'He's on trial with me. And my guess is he's not the back-stabbing type.'

A girl sucked her forefinger to wet it, dunked it in the pot of termites and then popped them into her mouth. 'Brain the size of a termite's,' she teased, licking her lips.

'He might not be as stupid as you think. We'll see.'

Lexi alternated between the bowl of crispy-fried bugs and the live food, pausing only to flick a carapace out from between her teeth.

Another girl exclaimed, 'You don't *like* him, do you? A major!'

Lexi shrugged. 'I doubt it. Too early to say. But I've known a lot worse.'

'Have you seen what they do after they've had a few drinks?'

'Hey. Just because I've got a major partner doesn't mean it's my job to defend them,' Lexi replied. 'But they're not the only ones who make a nuisance of themselves.'

'Have you heard – or seen – how their females go to the toilet? They sit down! Yes, they actually come into contact with it. Hygiene, please!'

Grimacing, Lexi said, 'So do the boys. On occasions.'

'Yuck.'

'Gross!'

Lexi laughed. 'And you know how they have children, don't you?'

Almost together, the outers cried, 'Don't go there!'

SCENE 8

Tuesday 8th April, Night

Grandma was tinkering around in the kitchen. 'How's it gone, honey?' she called out.

'Okay,' Troy answered.

'Is it an interesting case?'

Troy put his head round the door. 'You don't want to know the details.'

'Too true. And what about your partner? Do you get on okay with him?'

'Her.'

'*Her?*' Straining, she let out a grunt as she bent down to lift a large shepherd's pie from the oven.

Removing his jacket, Troy entered the kitchen with a smile on his face. 'Yes, *her*.'

'Oh, well. And is she … you know … an *outer*?'

'Yes. Lexi. She's cool.' He draped his coat over the back of a chair. 'Smells good,' he said. He hesitated and then added, 'The dinner, not Lexi.'

Grandma put the large dish down on the table and began to smother the meal in brown sauce. 'I've always thought it's best not to mix with outers.'

'They're just like us, Gran. Give or take the cooked cockroaches. Anyway,' he added, 'it's policy to pair up major and outer.'

'They commit most of the crime – and a lot of it's aimed at us,' said Grandma.

Troy had heard her opinion many times. It was a widely held view in the major community. He guessed that Lexi knew many outers who believed the exact opposite. 'It's not true, Gran. The figures say majors commit crimes against outers just as much as the other way round. Major-on-major and outer-on-outer crimes aren't exactly rare, either.'

'So you say.'

'That's why a major/outer pair looks into all serious crime,' Troy said. 'Better to form a duo than sing solo. And there's something else.'

'What's that, honey?'

'Sorry, but I've already eaten. With Lexi.'

'With Lexi, eh?' she replied, glancing at him. She didn't quite manage to disguise the hurt in her expression. 'I dread to think what was on the menu. Never mind. You can have your share tomorrow. It'll keep.'

SCENE 9

Wednesday 9th April, Morning

A counsellor had already broken the news to the Backhouse family that Dmitri's body had been found. Now, Troy wanted to talk to Dmitri's daughter, Coral. He felt that he could extract a clearer picture of Dmitri Backhouse from someone not far from his own age. But Coral was not at home. The counsellor had advised her to go into school as normal, because he believed that routine and lessons would take her mind off the terrible news about her father.

Shepford was laid out like most other cities. It had a commercial hub and concentric rings of neighbourhoods. At the city's heart were shops, the entertainment complex, industry, Crime Central, the temple, the sports centre and schools. Separated by strips of parkland, there were six zones of housing. Four were dominated by majors and two by outers.

Approaching Coral's school, it was clear to Troy and Lexi that there was a scuffle taking place between students on the playing field. When they were close enough to see what was going on, they realized that Coral Backhouse was at the heart of the punch-up. They both raced towards the brawl.

Blessed with superior fast-twitch muscles, outers were better sprinters, even if they didn't have the strength of majors. Lexi got to the fight first and waded in straightaway. Inside a circle of students, Coral was facing three outer girls and putting up a good fight, despite being outnumbered. Lexi grabbed the leading outer, locking her arms expertly behind her back. At the same time, she yelled, 'Oi! Stop. Detective!'

Troy arrived and grasped Coral in the same way, defusing the situation. 'Show over!' he shouted. 'Go on. Back to classes.'

'Except for you three,' Lexi said to the outer girls.

'And you, Coral,' Troy added.

Coral twisted round. 'How come you know me?'

'Photographs,' Troy said.

A teacher flew out of the nearest building and dashed towards the group. 'What's going on? Who are you? You can't just walk in here and ... ' Glancing at Lexi and Troy, he noticed their life-loggers and his protest faded away.

With a wry smile, Troy said, 'Oh, yes, we can.' He paused before adding, 'We need to talk to Coral. You can take the other three and get their side of the story.'

The teacher marched back towards the school building, shepherding the outer students.

Lexi laughed. 'You enjoyed that, didn't you?' she said to Troy. 'Overruling a teacher.'

Letting go of Coral, Troy admitted it. 'They told me what to do for years. Now it's my turn.' Then he faced Coral and asked, 'What was that all about?'

'Nothing,' she answered.

'I was always having fights like that – over nothing I'd admit to a teacher. But I'm not a teacher. My name's Troy, by the way. And you were giving it some welly with a nifty right-hand jab.'

Surly, she didn't reply.

'Let me guess,' said Troy. 'They were outers, right? And if they heard about your dad ... Were they teasing you about him?'

She didn't utter a word, but there was surprise in her eyes. She almost gasped at Troy's insight.

'Not all outers are like that,' Lexi told her. 'Not many at all.'

Coral glanced from Lexi to Troy. Apparently persuaded that she had a sympathetic audience, she muttered, 'The counsellor said he didn't kill himself.'

'It's true,' Troy replied. 'I'm sorry, but we're a murder investigation.'

She shook her head. 'It wasn't murder,' she insisted. 'He'd been threatening to do himself in for ages. I bet he got someone to do it for him.'

'That's still murder,' Troy told her. 'Have you got anyone in mind?'

'No. He didn't have any friends and no one in the family would've ... you know.'

'What about someone he'd met on the internet?'

'I don't know but, near the end, he spent a lot of time online. It's what he did instead of sleeping.'

'I'd like to get my hands on his computer,' said Lexi.

'Mum told the police. His laptop's gone. He took it with him, I suppose. All we know is, he called himself Backdown online.'

'How did you get on with him?' Troy asked.

'He wasn't the easiest ... I hated the long periods

of silence and panic attacks, but ... He's my dad. *Was* my dad, I mean.' Coral shrugged. 'No one gave me a choice.'

Troy nodded. 'You love what you get, though, don't you?'

'Sort of. Yeah.'

'You'd want to know who killed him and why.'

'Yes.'

'So,' Troy said, 'you can help me and Lexi sort it out. Think back to just before he disappeared. Anything unusual happen?'

'What sort of thing do you mean?'

Troy took a long breath. 'Anything. Maybe he said something strange. Any weird behaviour? Did you see him surfing any freaky sites?'

Coral leaned her head to one side while she thought. 'Well ... '

'What?'

'I lost my mobile and I was desperate to see an email. Dad wasn't around so I turned his laptop on. I didn't really look but there was a message about fishing.'

'Phishing with a ph,' Troy asked, 'or fishing with an f?'

'The watery sort. Only, I don't think he's ever done it before, so it was kind of freaky. But I thought ...

Whatever. It's not against the law if he wants to torture poor defenceless fish.'

Troy nodded slowly. 'Thanks. That's … interesting.'

Lexi glanced at her partner. He had clearly seen some link with the case.

'The message came from … I don't know, but Angel was part of the name. It caught my eye.'

'Charon Angel?'

'Something like that, yes.'

'That's useful as well,' said Troy.

'Is that it?' Coral asked. 'Because I'd better go in and find out how much trouble I'm in. By now, those girls will have made up all sorts about me.'

'You'll be fine,' Troy replied, 'after I've had a few words with the Head.'

'Will you?'

'Promise. You've been punished enough already.'

Before leaving, Troy told the head teacher about the death of Coral Backhouse's father. He insisted that Coral had been provoked into reacting. She needed support more than punishment.

Walking out of the school grounds with Lexi, Troy was still thinking about Coral's troubled relationship with her dad. He said, 'We're all victims of our parents' failings.'

'Not me,' Lexi replied. 'Not any outer.'

'Oh yes. What's it like not to have a real mum and dad?'

Lexi shrugged. 'What's it like to *have* a real mum and dad?'

Getting into the car, Troy didn't answer. Instead, he said, 'It must be weird to have paid people looking after you.'

'Huh. Professional nannies are paid because they're good at it. They don't have failings. A mum and dad might be rubbish at bringing up children. I doubt if Dmitri Backhouse was great.'

'Even so … '

Lexi butted in. 'Outers are cooperative breeders – we share out caring for our babies. You do it in families – even ones that aren't any good at it. You just let them get on with it, instead of changing things to make it better.'

Over the last few hundred years, the population of outers had crashed because outer women slowly lost the ability to carry a pregnancy. Their numbers began to increase again only when they learnt to reproduce differently. Compatible eggs and sperm were brought together in an artificial womb, nurtured into outer offspring and raised by nannies. For outers, friendship and romance were nothing to do with producing the next generation.

'Anyway,' Lexi added, 'what about *your* parents? What are their failings? What have they passed on to you?'

Uneasy, Troy glanced at her and said, 'Let's get back to the case.'

Lexi instructed the onboard computer, 'Shepford Crime Central.' Then she gazed at Troy for a few seconds before saying, 'All right. What's the fishing angle all about?'

'Look. I'm Dmitri Backhouse, thinking of killing myself. You're someone who knows about me from the internet and you want body parts. What are you going to do?'

'Set up a meeting.'

Troy nodded. 'Where?'

Lexi thought for a few seconds. 'Somewhere without witnesses or cameras.'

'Like the place where you go fishing. A reservoir with platforms at the edge, maybe.'

Lexi smiled. 'Okay. I see where you're going. But … '

'That'd be the reason you know it's a good place to bury a body. That'd be the connection I was after.'

'So what? Even if you're right, how does it help?'

'I'm no expert,' Troy replied, 'but I think you need a licence to go fishing.'

'So you want a list of everyone around here with a fishing licence that covers Langhorn Reservoir?'

'Exactly.'

'What if this internet friend's fishing illegally – without one?'

'I just think he'll have one. He wouldn't want to draw attention to himself – or *herself* – by getting caught for something trivial.'

'We'll see.'

'If we got a list, I bet you'd want to examine all their shoes.'

'That could be hundreds – or even thousands. Anyway ... '

'What?'

'It's all speculation,' said Lexi, as the car pulled up outside Crime Central.

'True,' Troy agreed. 'Maybe it's a stick I've grasped the wrong end of.' He shrugged. 'It's down to your fancy forensics to prove me wrong or right.'

SCENE 10

Wednesday 9th April, Midday

'I've got a list of people with fishing licences for the Shepford area,' Lexi reported. 'But I'm told Langhorn Reservoir isn't very popular. There are far better places, apparently.'

'That fits. Our fishing fanatic, suicide chat room stalker and body part trader wouldn't get disturbed by other people if it's out of favour.'

'He's a fictional fishing fanatic, suicide chat room stalker and body part trader at the moment.'

'I'm working on it.' Grinning, Troy added, 'I'm fishing as well. Casting about in a suicide forum.'

'Caught anything?'

'A few sympathetic posts. Nothing out of the ordinary. I'm going to try again.' He spoke as he typed. *'No one even notices me and what I do. I might as well not exist.'*

With a wicked expression, Lexi replied, 'Very believable. It's a cry that could come from any major.'

Spinning his chair round towards her, Troy ignored her comment. 'So, how many people hold fishing licences around here?'

'Too many. Hundreds. If one of them's our killer, we need to filter out a lot of others first. I could use foot size, but we don't have grounds for going round checking people's shoes and treads. We'd be doing it on a wild hunch.'

'And I suppose we don't know for certain that the shoeprints belong to the bad guy.' Troy hesitated and then said, 'Is there a Huw on the list?'

'No.'

'That fits as well. He's not the sort to bother with a licence. Are any of them Dr Something? Like a transplant surgeon?'

'I thought you'd never ask. We've got two doctors who go fishing. Neither's got anything to do with transplants, though. I've already checked. One's a doctor of physics and the other's a retired baby specialist.'

Disappointed, Troy glanced at his computer screen and uttered a little cry. 'Hey. Charon Angel's online again. Remember? Coral said someone called Angel left her dad a message as well. Listen. "No one is worthless. Even if it seems that way. You have value."'

Suddenly interested, Lexi said, 'You should put, *I'm probably worth more dead than alive.*'

'Let's make a deal,' Troy replied with a smile. 'I won't tell you how to analyse clues if you don't tell me how to handle suspects.'

'What's wrong with what I said?'

'It's too obvious. If Charon's running a scam for spare parts, he's going to be suspicious. You'd make it sound like I'm setting a trap. We've got to be more ... '

'Crafty?'

'Yes.' As Troy typed, he said aloud, *'Thanks, Charon. I'm tired of visitors just telling me not to do it. You put a different slant on it. But I feel like I'm dead already. All that remains is to make it official.'*

'Don't rush into anything,' Charon Angel replied at once.

'If I've made my mind up,' Troy typed, *'why not?'*

'Because I might be able to help,' came the response.

'What do you mean? What sort of help?'

'I might be able to help you realize your value.'

Troy looked up at Lexi. 'Tricky, isn't it? He might be trying to persuade me I have a worthwhile life, or he might be working out how much cash he's going to make after he's helped me die.'

'It's your crazy language again,' Lexi complained. 'It's down to how you interpret "realize your value". How are you going to find out which he means?'

Troy hesitated. 'I don't want to ask to meet him. I want to see if *he* does that.' Turning back to the keypad, he wrote, *'I'll think about it.'*

There was a delay of a few seconds before the reply appeared on screen. *'Thinking before acting is wise. You can't do it afterwards. I'll look out for you on this site. If you come back, I'll be here. Remember: there are always people who care – and who benefit from you.'*

Turning away, Troy muttered, 'He's right. There's probably a queue of transplant patients.'

'Charon Angel must know that you – or anyone else – could just volunteer to be an organ donor,' Lexi said. 'Giving your bits and pieces for nothing.'

Troy nodded. 'Not enough do, I suppose. That's why there's a black market. Anyway, if Charon's in that game, he wouldn't want me to give my heart or anything else away. Perhaps he'd persuade me the money would come in useful for family or friends – or some cause I believe in. Then, after I'm gone, he'd run off with it.' Troy twisted round and logged out of the chat room. 'I want to play hard to get. I want him – or her – to sweat for a bit.'

'Everything they've written could be innocent,' Lexi said. 'They might genuinely be worried about you.'

'*They*?'

'I know,' Lexi said. 'It's not my fault, though. It's the language again. If you don't know whether someone's a *he* or a *she* in English, a lot of people just say "they" instead. I do it myself sometimes. "They" can mean one person! Ridiculous. On top of that, it can mean just about anybody as well. When someone says, "They've arrested your best friend", it means *us*: the police or detectives. But you've got to figure it out for yourself. "They say it's going to rain" means weather forecasters.' Frustrated, she shook her head.

'It might mean old folk like my grandma, who says she can feel it in her bones.'

'Quite. Not a clue.'

'Anyway,' said Troy, 'I'm stopping for a bit because it gives us time to find out who the site administrator is.'

'You're hoping they'll tell us who Charon Angel is.'

'Exactly.'

They both began to check out databases and directories.

After half an hour of research, Lexi announced, 'I told you I was the methodical one. The administrator's called Sergio Treize, based in ... Switzerland.'

'Switzerland?' Troy exclaimed. 'Excellent. The world's best chocolate. I'll grab my skis.'

Lexi smiled. 'Don't bother. Our laws don't stretch that far. If he doesn't want to cooperate, he doesn't have to.'

Tapping the computer screen, Troy said, 'You've got enough info here for me to put in a video call. What time is it in Switzerland?'

'I think they're an hour ahead of us,' Lexi answered.

'That's all right then.'

The first three attempts failed, but Troy got through to Sergio Treize at the fourth try. The outer's head, shoulders and chest were displayed on Troy's screen. In his thirties, he wore a sweatshirt with an abstract image and logo, prominent white-rimmed spectacles and he was bald. Oddly, he shook his head from side to side at least twice every minute, giving the impression of trying to dislodge a fly from his cheek without using a hand. Troy assumed he had a nervous tic.

With his computer recording the video conversation, Troy introduced himself.

'So,' Sergio said in a French accent, 'you're a detective.' His words and movements were not quite synchronized by the technology.

'Yes. Investigating a possible assisted suicide.'

'Is that a crime?'

'Over here, yes.' After a brief pause, Troy added, 'As you'll know.'

'I'm aware of several overseas people using my services because they've got no local equivalents.'

'I'm interested in the chat room.'

Sergio's head gave another nervous shake. 'It's very comforting for those who need it.'

'There's a contributor called Charon Angel.'

'Is there?'

'Yes,' Troy replied. 'I need to know who he or she is.'

'The site guarantees anonymity.'

'No one deserves a guarantee if they take advantage of people at real low points.'

'What makes you think ... ' Sergio hesitated. Clearly, he'd forgotten the username.

'Charon Angel.'

'Yes. What makes you think Charon Angel has been abusing the site – and the people who visit it?'

'I reckon he's scouting for body parts.'

'What?' Sergio cried, visibly shocked.

'For medical transplants,' Troy explained.

'I find that hard to believe.' Sergio turned his head to the side and stroked his chin for a few seconds. 'I'm looking at his contributions now. I can't see anything definite. He's either a perfectly good visitor – in which case you don't need his name – or you're right and he'll have supplied a false name and details. Either way, it won't help you to hand over his profile, so I'm ending this call.'

'Just tell me. Is he in Switzerland, over here, or somewhere else?'

'He's in Switzerland.'

'Thanks,' Troy said. 'Why don't you keep an eye on what he does? If he posts anything suspicious, send me as much information as you can. All right?'

Sergio shrugged. 'I'm a busy man, but I'll monitor him. And, by that, I mean him or her.'

As soon as the image on the screen faded, Troy said to Lexi, 'Who's the best computer geek in Crime Central? I've got a hacking job I want doing.'

SCENE 11

Wednesday 9th April, Afternoon

April showers had not yet arrived. Lying down on the dry ground beside the last line of trees, Lexi raised the binoculars to her eyes and focused on the left-hand side of the Rural Retreat Transplant Clinic. Then she glanced down at the plan of the building that she'd unearthed and spread it out on the soil. 'There's no obvious basement,' she whispered, 'but there's a whole wing Gianna Humble didn't take us into.'

'She never said she'd show us everything,' Troy replied. 'Maybe that's where the clean rooms and operating theatres are. No one but doctors and patients would be allowed in. And everyone would have to be scrubbed up.'

A private ambulance came to a halt at the front of the clinic. There was no siren, no panic. A couple of nurses opened the back doors and carefully extracted a patient on a stretcher. Wheeled legs unfolded automatically from underneath the carrier as it emerged from the vehicle, allowing a smooth and effortless transfer to the treatment centre.

Attached to a convenient tree trunk, Lexi's tiny spy camera recorded all of the comings and goings at the main entrance.

Lexi nodded towards the new arrival and said, 'That's one thing I've come for.'

Troy looked puzzled. 'The patient, ambulance, or the trolley?'

'I think it's called a gurney. Saying *trolley* makes it sound like supermarket shopping. Anyway, I need to get my hands on one before we go.'

'Why?'

'You'll see.'

'Are we going to the back to set up another camera?'

'Yeah,' she answered. 'Keep low so no one sees us.'

They stayed out of view of the clinic until they

were at the edge of the wood opposite the rear entrance. Lexi fixed her second miniature camera to a branch, giving her a clear view of the area where body parts were delivered.

'That's done,' she announced as she crouched down next to her partner. 'It'll be interesting to see what arrives in the next few days. Let's go back round to the front. I want to check out what you call a trolley.'

'Okay.'

When they reached the spot where Lexi had attached the first spy camera, they squatted down again. After a while, a nurse came out of the clinic, pushing the gurney. She left it near the ambulance and went back in through the automatic door.

Seeing an opportunity, Lexi began to scramble to her feet.

Troy's arm shot out. He grabbed the sleeve of her jacket and yanked her back down.

'What ... ?' she said in an urgent whisper.

'Look.'

A man wearing a suit and a peaked cap had appeared outside the clinic.

'So?' said Lexi. 'It doesn't matter who sees me now. I'm not going to break in or anything. I'm just going to measure a gurney.'

'I saw him here yesterday,' Troy told her as he watched the well-built man walk towards a cab. 'Don't you think it's weird to be that smart and top it off with a baseball cap?'

'Yes,' she replied, 'but probably not illegal. Shall I get onto the fashion police and see what they think?'

Troy smiled wryly. 'No. I want to find out who he is.'

Lexi nodded towards the camera. 'You'll have his picture to help.'

Pointing at the cab, Troy said, 'That's even better.' He checked the exact time on his life-logger.

Standing up and brushing the dirt from her sleeves and trouser legs, Lexi said, 'I've got a job to do.'

From the edge of the wood, Troy watched Lexi while he spoke into his phone. 'Travel? Yes. I've just watched a middle-aged man take a cab from the Rural Retreat Transplant Clinic. At fifteen twenty-seven precisely. Can you trace it? I want his name and where he's going. Thanks.'

When Lexi bent down and measured the width of gurney wheels and the distance between them, Troy realized what was on his partner's mind. He nodded his approval.

When she returned, she said, 'The wheels are fifty-four centimetres apart. That's two more than the tracks in the field by the bodies. So that's that. Our guy didn't use a gurney from here.'

'Not if they're all the same.'

'I bet they are – so they all fit the equipment in the ambulance and inside the hospital. I'm after some other type of cart. It might not have anything to do with health and hospitals. The transplant trade isn't the only explanation for our dead bodies.'

Troy hadn't forgotten that a peculiar and cruel operation might lie behind the death of the female major with an outer heart. But he couldn't make sense of it. He understood the need for transplants. He could even believe that mistakes might happen. But he couldn't work out the motive behind a deliberate biological mix-up. 'Why would anyone put outer organs in majors? Or the other way round?'

Lexi shivered violently. 'Maybe it was an experiment to make a sort of outer-major hybrid.'

'What?' Troy exclaimed.

'I know. It's not natural. It's ... No. Horrible thought.'

Troy shook his head, dismissing the idea. 'Are you done here?'

'For now,' she answered. 'Let's go and leave the cameras to do their job.'

As they walked towards the car, Crime Central's

Travel Section called Troy. 'The man you're after, his name is Dylan Farthing and he's on his way home.'

'Which is … where?'

'Shepford third quarter. Fifteen Ennis Street.'

'Great. Thanks.'

In the car, Troy said, 'Fifteen Ennis Street, Shepford,' and the onboard computer took control of the journey.

Lexi shook her head. 'You're going after him, why? Because he looks shady?'

'Because I'm curious. And he's got the muscles you'd need to lug dead bodies around.'

'I'll get the handcuffs ready – in case we come across any other body-builders,' said Lexi. 'They're into killing people and mutilating their bodies.'

Ignoring her sarcasm, Troy replied, 'You can check his shoe size.'

SCENE 12

Wednesday 9th April, Late afternoon

Ennis Street looked familiar. Troy had probably never been there, but it was the standard design for Shepford's third quarter. The neat detached houses were a uniform light brown colour, built from the same local stone. They were all similarly sized boxes, two storeys high with tiled roofs that sloped from left to right. Each had a small front garden and a larger one at the rear.

Troy pushed the doorbell at number fifteen. After a few seconds, the smart and sturdy man appeared in front of him. This time there was no cap, but he was wearing tinted spectacles that also seemed out of place. 'Yes?' he said, glancing at the life-loggers attached to his visitors' waists.

Troy asked, 'Are you Dylan Farthing?'

'That's me.'

'Good. Detectives Troy Goodhart and Lexi Four. We've got a few questions for you. Can we come in?'

Dylan stood to one side of the hall, next to a small table. 'What's this about?'

As they walked into the plain, spotless living room, Troy replied, 'We're looking into some events near the Rural Retreat Transplant Clinic – and we know you go there. We wondered if you'd seen anything useful to our investigation.'

With cropped fair hair instead of a baseball cap, he looked very different. 'Like what?'

'Well, first, perhaps I'd better ask why you go to the clinic.'

Dylan sighed. 'Isn't it obvious?'

'Not to me,' said Troy. 'Sorry.'

He touched his dark glasses. 'Why do you think I wear these? Why do I need a stupid cap outside? Why go to the clinic? I've just had a cornea transplant in my left eye and I have to protect it from sunlight.'

'Right. But as you went to and from the clinic, did you see ... ?'

'I saw hardly anything. That's why I needed the operation.'

Troy expected Lexi to be sneering at him but, when he glanced at her, she wasn't. She was gazing down at the freshly vacuumed carpet. Troy decided that a rapid retreat was the best policy. Heading for the door, he said to Dylan, 'Well, I'm sorry to bother you. I wouldn't have if I'd known about your condition.'

As they walked away, Troy waited for a cutting comment from Lexi, but it didn't come. Inside the car, he said, 'You seem … thoughtful.'

'Yeah.'

'And … ?'

Plugging her life-logger into her laptop, she said, 'I liked his carpet. Clean with a nice pile.'

'So?' Troy prompted.

'We all leave clear footprints on a carpet after it's been vacuumed.'

'You recorded his?'

'Larger than average, standard leather shoe.' She showed Troy the imprint on the laptop screen. With her forefinger, she marked the position of the toe. Then she slid her finger across the image to the heel and a cursor followed her movement. She lingered for a moment on the back of the shoeprint. At once, the measurement appeared alongside the cursor: *29.5 cm*. 'Thought so,' she muttered. 'Size twelve.'

'But not the same as the trainer near the bodies.'

'No,' she replied.

Troy regretted that majors and outers wore the same types and sizes of shoe – and walked in the same way. The two human races could not be distinguished by their footwear.

'I'd write it off as a coincidence,' Lexi continued. 'But ... '

'What?'

'There was a letter on the little table in the hall. Addressed to Farthing Family Butchers.'

'He's a butcher?'

'Meaning he knows his way around a dead body. And he's handy with a sharp knife.'

SCENE 13

Wednesday 9th April, Early evening

'Tomorrow night feels right. I am content. I'm ready. Everything's in place. It's a good time to go.'

Troy sat back, checked what he'd written and smiled. 'That's a cat I'm putting among the pigeons.'

Lexi shook her head. 'Sometimes you talk in riddles.'

'It'll force Charon Angel's hand,' said Troy, hitting the return key to post the comment online.

Replies began to arrive within a minute.

'I implore you to seek help.'

'What you're thinking of doing is wrong. The taking of any life is against God's law. Choose life.'

'Forget the past. Whatever happened there is over. You must look to the future and recognize its potential. Start afresh.'

After three minutes came the message that Troy most wanted to see. Charon Angel wrote, *'The day after tomorrow – or next week, next month or whatever – some full-of-life girl might step off the road in front of a speeding cab. You might have been the one person close enough to yank her back, to save her life. Perhaps she would have gone on to be a leading politician, making the world a better place. That's what I meant about you – and everyone else – having unknown value. If you go ahead, your absence will change the way things are supposed to be. It's a shame to deny the world your contribution.'*

Troy let out a sigh and shut his eyes for a few seconds. 'His tone's changed,' he muttered. 'Why?'

'I don't know,' Lexi replied, 'But he's in the clear. "It's a shame to deny the world your contribution." That's no way for anyone to get their hands on your kidneys.'

Troy nodded slowly. 'Unless Sergio Treize tipped him off. Warned him we're watching. Now he's coming over all innocent.'

'That's a bit devious.'

'But possible.'

'Maybe it's just you getting desperate for a suspect,' Lexi said.

'Not desperate. Imaginative,' Troy replied with a grin. 'Don't forget I'm the perceptive one.'

Lexi checked out an incoming message on her life-logger and then said, 'We'll see. Terabyte's on his way.'

The computer technician had a real name but no one used it. A lot of the people who asked for Terabyte's help didn't even know what he was actually called.

He'd first made a name for himself at school. He'd won himself and every other student a two-day holiday in winter with an electronic attack on the building's computerized heating system. One of his mates congratulated him a little too loudly for freezing everyone out of school. A teacher overheard and, from then on, everyone became aware of his special skills.

Now, at the age of seventeen, he was Crime Central's best computer nerd. And Troy had asked him to gate-crash the administration of the suicide website.

He came into the room, sneezed, flung his hair over one shoulder and adjusted the glasses on his nose. 'I hacked into better-protected sites when I was ten,' he said.

'So,' Troy replied, trying to control his rising expectation, 'you've found out all about Charon Angel.'

'Pretty much,' he replied. 'Her name is Sharon Angie.'

'It's a she?'

'I haven't seen a photo but Sharon sounds female to me. The site admin doesn't have a lot on her, but she's living in Switzerland. Way up a mountain in a village called Wengen. I've got her email address, not a house address. Or cottage, or whatever they have in Wengen.'

'Anything else? How old is she? Has she been to this country?'

'I trawled around. According to Passport Control, she's never been here. She's twenty-seven and she shops a lot online. I don't suppose they've got supermarkets at the top of Swiss mountains. Again, no home address, but judging by what she's been buying, she likes books on psychology and martial arts, music from Iceland, wine and car maintenance.' Terabyte had a long and cute face. When his hair flopped forward, he gave the impression of a spaniel.

Troy's shoulders dropped and his enthusiasm

faded. Terabyte had just blown his theory that Charon Angel was hunting body parts. She hadn't even been in the country. What had happened to Troy's usually reliable instinct?

'I'm guessing I've disappointed you,' said Terabyte.

Troy nodded. 'That's me done for today. I've got a shepherd's pie waiting at home. With bucketfuls of brown sauce.'

Terabyte looked at Lexi with a grin on his face. 'Us outers wouldn't know if shepherds taste nice with or without sauce.'

SCENE 14

Monday 7th April, Early afternoon

Lexi gazed at her life-logger and groaned. 'That's another avenue blocked off. Only a couple of people have had hand transplants and they both check out. Done in genuine hospitals with genuine hands donated by genuine accident victims.'

With a wide grin, Troy said, 'Nothing underhand going on there, then.'

Lexi groaned again.

Troy apologised for the joke. 'I'm not surprised you didn't turn anything up. It fits. If Dmitri got involved with some sort of medical black market, the transplant wouldn't be officially registered.' He shrugged. 'Let's face it. Right now we're a bit stumped with Dmitri and L4G#1. Let's not make them brick walls for banging our heads against. Let's tackle the major woman with the wrong heart, L4G#2.' Troy was still pained to refer to two of the bodies by codes rather than names, but he had no choice until he discovered their identities. 'I've been thinking about it overnight.'

'Oh?' Lexi took a careful bite out of a block of soft, decomposing cheese. It was casu marzu, crawling with live insect larvae. If jolted, the maggots would launch themselves about fifteen centimetres away and she'd lose their juicy flavour.

'As far as we know, no one's reported her missing. So, maybe she lived on her own. Why don't we put out a call to shops and anyone who delivers things to people's houses? Is anyone supplying things to what appears to be an empty house? Is stuff piling up at the door?'

'Sounds reasonable.' Fiddling with her life-logger, Lexi said, 'I'll do it.'

'What about your spy cameras outside the transplant clinic?'

'I looked at the footage last night and this morning – between meditations. Nothing iffy. No unmarked vans pulling up to the doors. Just the comings and goings you'd expect for a legitimate health centre. Gianna Humble, Blade Five, nurses, cleaners, a couple of patients.'

Sucking on a chunk of mint chocolate, Troy nodded. 'Imagine I run a shady transplant outfit. I've got some embarrassing bodies to get rid of. I might well do it near a proper clinic, so it got the blame if someone found what I'd buried.'

'It's a possibility, I suppose,' she admitted.

'Have forensics found anything interesting in all that stuff they took from the wood?'

'Nothing that definitely links to the case.'

SCENE 15

Thursday 10th April, Late morning

Goods had indeed piled up outside the large, posh house on the edge of Shepford. The trader who made the regular deliveries had recently become suspicious and had wandered round to the back garden. When she'd spotted a broken window, she'd reported it to Crime Central. At once, Troy and Lexi upgraded the low-priority incident at Olga Wylie's house to the highest priority.

Troy almost tiptoed through the house. That seemed appropriate and respectful, in case he was now invading a dead woman's personal space.

'No evidence of anyone else living here,' Lexi called out, less sensitive than Troy.

'I think we can class Olga Wylie as rich and a loner,' Troy whispered.

They were in her study – the room with a broken window. Lexi examined the dust on the desk. 'There used to be something on here. Something about the size of a laptop. And, look, an electric cable for charging a computer battery. But nothing to plug it into.'

Troy nodded. 'Someone broke in and took it, then?'

'Maybe.' Lexi bagged some dust because she knew it would contain human skin. With tweezers, she also picked up a hair with a root. She'd extract DNA from both.

'Just like Dmitri Backhouse. No computer. If I'm right, it means there was something significant on it. When she died, someone got rid of it.'

'I've got a visible fingerprint here,' Lexi said. Checking on her life-logger for a few seconds, she added, 'Eighty-four per cent match with L4G#2. It's not perfect because the body was degraded. Assuming this,' she said, pointing to the pattern in the dust, 'belongs to Olga Wylie, we've got a name for our second body.'

Sad, but relieved, Troy nodded again. He requested Olga's medical details and then soaked up the atmosphere while his partner went about her job. Not much seemed to have been disturbed. The burglar hadn't ransacked the place. That suggested he or she came in for something specific – like Olga's computer.

Lexi went over to the smashed window and peered closely at it. Then she examined the carpet underneath. Disappointed, she said, 'I can't see any blood, fibres or anything from the burglar. We'll need a detailed search and special equipment. That might show up some traces.'

'They're like chickens. Not to be counted till they hatch.'

Lexi did not look up. 'Don't worry. If I don't get anything on the person who smashed the window, I'll find something else. All it takes is for me to be more thorough than the guy who broke in. Shouldn't be a problem. I'll get the forensic team to go over the place millimetre by millimetre, if necessary. Every drawer, every nook and cranny.'

Troy didn't know his partner very well yet, but he had every confidence in her already. He accompanied her as she went methodically from room to room, making notes, using her life-logger. Troy built up a different kind of picture of Olga Wylie. There were no photographs on the walls, no signs of a fondness for family or friends. No signs of fondness for herself. There was one photograph of Olga. It was lying face-down in the living room. Along with the contents of her kitchen, it told Troy that she was an overweight middle-aged woman who ate too much junk food and drank alcohol. Perhaps her lifestyle had contributed to her ill-health. At least the photo confirmed that she was L4G#2.

When Lexi had been in every room, she stopped and said, 'You know one thing we haven't found?'

'A computer.'

'Apart from that.'

'What?'

'Her handbag.'

'Handbag?'

Lexi smiled. 'An essential piece of equipment for major women. They keep all sorts in them. Rummage in a handbag and you'll find a forensic treasure trove.'

'So, what do we do?'

'We go round again – till we find it. And if we don't, I put the whole team on the job. Come on. It'll be tucked away somewhere, but easily accessible. Perhaps with her coats, so she could grab both at the same time.'

Lexi went out into the hall, examining every door, every surface, even tapping the walls and listening to the sound. She found what she wanted under the stairs. The wall panel sounded hollow. There was no obvious way into the cubby-hole, no handle. On the left-hand side, the door didn't react to Lexi's push. But when she touched the right-hand side of the panel, it sprang back smoothly.

Reaching inside, Lexi cried, 'Hey presto! Coats and handbag. We're in business.' She put the embroidered bag down on a table, opened it and delved inside. As an outer, she could never leave fingerprints on evidence, but she used gloves to avoid contaminating it with flakes of her skin and smudging traces with sweat. 'Here we go,' she declared, lifting out a smartphone. 'Not as good as a laptop, but I want Terabyte on this.'

SCENE 16

Thursday 10th April, Afternoon

Terabyte had synchronized Olga Wylie's mobile with his computer. His monitor showed exactly what was on her smartphone. He'd got a short list of phone numbers that she'd used, a very brief history of texts and a record of internet sites that she'd visited. The phone had not recorded any activity after Tuesday 25th March.

'Just over two weeks ago,' said Troy. 'That's probably when she died.' He touched his life-logger and said, 'I got her medical records. She had a weak heart. She'd been on the transplant waiting list for ages but she didn't get lucky. No one donated a heart that matched her blood type. No one legal anyway.'

'All these phone numbers and texts check out,' Terabyte told the two detectives. 'Nothing shifty. A hairdresser, the online shop she used, the hospital … '

'Genuine hospital?' asked Troy.

'Yes. And the texts are from a bank, shops and that sort of thing. Her emails have been deleted. Not a single one left.'

Troy sighed. 'Okay. Let's see the internet sites in her history.'

Terabyte displayed them on his monitor.

Almost immediately, Troy picked out one from the small number of named sites. She'd visited 'The Solitude Network' repeatedly. 'What's that?'

Terabyte clicked on the link and read from the header, 'A place for the lonely and isolated to meet and talk.'

'That's what we want,' Troy declared immediately. 'We need to know who she's been talking to.'

'We don't know her username.'

'True,' Troy replied, 'but I want to see every message on the site for … let's say … a month leading up to 25th March.'

'Sure,' Terabyte said. 'No problem.' He stroked a few keys and the information appeared onscreen.

Scrolling down the sizeable blog, he muttered, 'There's a lot of lonely people out there.'

'If Olga posted anything, we might be able to work out which one she is, what she put and what replies she got,' said Troy eagerly. 'We can narrow it down by eliminating anybody who blogged after 25th March.'

'And the ones who are obviously men or outers,' Lexi said.

'Okay. I'm on to it,' Terabyte replied. His fingers flew across the keypad and the onscreen list began to shorten.

'Hold it!' Lexi almost shouted.

'What?'

She pointed to an entry on the screen. 'A post by someone calling themselves Wily Fox. Is that a coincidence? We're after Olga Wylie.'

Troy said, 'No, it's not a coincidence. Look. It's about health and hearts.'

Samaritan 999: *I've been thinking. What about alternative medicine? Have you tried anything like that?*

Wily Fox: *I've heard of the crazy stuff like powdered rhino horn. That's supposed to reduce fevers, but I just think of the poor creatures that get killed. Does any of it really work? Are there any that heal hearts without hurting animals?*

Samaritan 999: *Let me do a bit of research. I think there is something. Maybe I can put you in touch with someone who could help.*

Wily Fox: *Thanks. I'll log back on tomorrow.*

Troy said, 'Scroll back in time, Terabyte. She must have blogged about her heart problem before. Can you isolate all her posts – and the replies?'

'That's a manual sorting job. It'll take a while.'

'How long? Hours?'

Terabyte shrugged. 'It depends how much there is. But, no, I mean minutes, not seconds.'

'You're a genius.'

'I know,' Terabyte replied. 'But I'll get it onto your life-loggers quicker if you're not breathing down my neck and talking to me.'

'Hint taken. We'll leave you to it.' Pushing his luck on his way out, Troy said, 'Afterwards, you could contact whoever hosts this site. See if they'll tell you anything about Wily Fox and Samaritan 999.'

'Okay.'

'Thanks.'

Walking away with Troy, Lexi said, 'Some spare minutes. Great. I'm going to switch off. I guess you're going to do the opposite.'

Troy nodded. 'Thinking time.'

Half an hour later, they were both reading Olga's entries on The Solitude Network. Quickly, they focused on the posts that had something to do with her health and read the first one.

Wily Fox: *Normally I don't mind being on my own. Love it really. I'm not your typical lonely heart and I'm not after a date. It's just that there are times when it would be great to have someone to sympathise.*

Take a Break: *I'm with you on that, Wily Fox. What's the problem?*

Wily Fox: *Illness, I'm afraid.*

Take a Break: *I know precisely what you mean.*

Samaritan 999: *Me too. Is it the silly niggling things or something serious that gets you down?*

Wily Fox: *Let me put it this way. I'm not so much a lonely heart as a failing heart.*

Samaritan 999: *That's not so good.*

Take a Break: *You have plenty of sympathy here. Virtual hugs and kisses.*

'The follow-up chat was interesting,' Troy said. 'The bit about alternative medicine and putting her in touch with someone who could help.'

'Yeah. I wonder what Samaritan 999 means by "alternative". If your heart's clapped out, that's it. You need a new one. A few herbs won't fix it.'

Troy agreed. 'I think Samaritan 999's trying to be

subtle, nudging her towards the black market in new hearts. That's definitely alternative. And she could afford it all right.' He turned back to the screen. 'Where did they go afterwards?'

Wily Fox: *Breathless and tired today. Nothing from the hospital.*

Samaritan 999: *What are you actually waiting for?*

Wily Fox: *A heart. I mean a real heart. I'm not talking about courage. Though courage would be good as well.*

Samaritan 999: *A transplant?*

Wily Fox: *Yes. Apparently I've exhausted all other treatments.*

Samaritan 999: *Maybe I can help. My friends in the alternative medicine business have a transplant clinic. It's not free, though.*

Wily Fox: *Money's not a problem. I just want a normal life.*

Take a Break: *Be careful, Wily Fox. There are some dodgy doctors out there.*

Wily Fox: *But I don't have long if nothing's done. Desperate situations call for desperate measures. I'll try anything.*

Samaritan 999: *If you send me your email, I can fix you up.*

[Next entry deleted for a breach of security rules: email address detected.]

Troy sat back in his chair. 'Now that's a cat let out of the bag. I think we can assume Olga got in touch and used her cash to jump the queue. She had a transplant in some rogue clinic. Things went horribly wrong and she got an outer's heart. Then this underground organization tried to cover it up by burying the evidence, knowing she was a loner. They reckoned no one would come looking for her.'

Lexi nodded. 'Can't fault the logic. And it reminds me of Dmitri Backhouse arranging things through a chat room.'

'I'd like to meet Samaritan 999 and Charon Angel. One trawls for lonely people that no one will miss and the other stalks possible suicides online. Maybe they're the same person.'

'Huh. Don't forget Charon Angel – that's Sharon Angie – came across as perfectly innocent in her last message.'

Troy hesitated before replying. 'Don't you forget Sergio Treize could have told her a detective's prowling around. Maybe that's why she changed.'

'But if you live in Switzerland, you can't murder people in Shepford. And that's that.'

Lexi's life-logger vibrated with news from Olga Wylie's house. The forensic examination was continuing but the team had found evidence of the intruder. A single faint impression in the flower bed at the side of the house matched Unknown Shoeprint 1 left by the burial site in the wood. Size 12, trainer-type, with Adibok's logo incorporated into the design of the tread. She looked up at Troy and asked, 'How many women – outer or major – do you know who wear size twelve shoes? That's 29.6 cm from toe to heel.'

Troy shrugged. 'Probably none.'

'Okay. It's almost certainly a man. He's been near where the bodies were buried and now he's been poking around Olga Wylie's house.' She paused before adding, 'Time I went back to the wood.'

SCENE 17

Thursday 10th April, Late afternoon

The log cabin in the wood seemed to be deserted. 'Huw!' Lexi shouted loudly. 'Hello?'

No reply. Just the sound of birds calling.

'Not here,' Troy said. 'Which doesn't mean a lot on its own, but … '

'What?'

'Everything's exactly the same as it was on Tuesday,' Troy observed.

The large axe and fishing rod were still propped against the cabin wall and most of Huw's woodworking tools were still laid out on the table.

Lexi glanced around. 'Now you mention it … '

'That's a spanner thrown in the works. If he's gone, is he another victim or a suspect we've scared off?'

'He's a suspect if he's got size twelve feet. A very strong one. That's why I'm here. To find out.' Staring at the ground, Lexi took a deep breath. 'No, I don't think so.' She pointed her life-logger at a clear impression of a left boot outside the cabin door and then said, 'Small feet. Size eight. And a match with Unknown Shoeprint 2. The one with a bit of rubber chipped off.' She sighed. 'All that proves is he wanders around the wood. But he could be an accomplice. He helped out here with the bodies but didn't go to Olga's.'

'Possible,' Troy replied. 'But I saw him as a loner, a free spirit, not partnering anyone.'

'More likely a victim, then.'

'For his sake, I hope he's neither. Maybe he just didn't like the intrusion. You and me asking questions and a forensic team trampling over what he'd see as his territory. Maybe he's just upped and off. I don't suppose it takes him long to plan a move. Not a lot to pack.' Troy took his life-logger in his hand and said, 'I'll still get a team to go through the wood, looking for fresh digging.'

'Talking of people on the move, I'll get someone to find out if Olga bought any travel tickets just before 25th March. No doubt we'd be interested in where she went.'

Walking back towards the car parked in the narrow lane, Troy said, 'It's sad, isn't it? We – the people – shouldn't need laws at all. We shouldn't have to be told it's bad to be nasty to each other. It should be pretty obvious.'

'I suppose.'

'You'd think us humans would know what's right and what's wrong. Especially majors.'

'Why especially majors?' Lexi asked with a frown.

'We've got an inbuilt brake on behaviour – our religious code.'

'You don't need a god to be nice to each other,' Lexi objected. 'Everyone's got moral instinct. Outers included. We all know killing and removing someone's organs is a bad thing to do. Anyway,' she added, clearly offended, 'even with all that religion, majors do horrible things.'

Troy nodded. 'What do you think would happen if we got rid of you and me – the law – tomorrow?'

Shrugging, Lexi said, 'All countries have laws. That tells me everywhere goes crazy without them.'

'That's what I mean. It's really sad.'

'I guess ninety-nine per cent of people would still be nice to each other.'

'That leaves one per cent who'd turn us into a lawless mess. One per cent too many.'

Reaching the car, its door unlocked for Lexi. 'Let's ignore the one per cent right now,' she said, 'and just concentrate on one person. Our bad guy.'

Settling inside, both of their mobiles began to ring at the same time. The caller was the same as well. Terabyte.

'Hi,' Lexi said. 'How did you … ?'

'I'm a genius with phones as well. Anyway, I wanted to speak to both of you. I got hold of The Solitude Network supervisor. After Samaritan 999's last chat with Wily Fox, he was banned from the site. He kept asking for contact details of people who didn't want a date. Three strikes and you're out, apparently. A waste of time if you ask me. He could log in from a different device under a different username.'

Eagerly, Troy asked, 'Did you get any info on him – or her?'

'Admin weren't as protective as they usually are – maybe because he'd been a bad boy and got booted off. Anyway, he ticked the bloke box, registered with an email that he abandoned straight after, and gave a false name and address. That's another breach of the site's rules.'

'Not much help, then,' said Troy.

'Did you follow up any of the visitors he'd tried to meet? Meet in reality, I mean, not virtual get-togethers,' Lexi said. 'Because if he succeeded, they could be victims as well. And we've got at least one more casualty – L4G#4 – an outer whose heart ended up in a major.'

'Of course I followed up,' Terabyte replied, as if insulted by her question. 'I couldn't get any personal information but – here's the big news – two of them logged on from Foreditch Homeless Centre. No idea what they posted or when they did it, but the place is about forty kilometres away from where you are right now.'

'Thanks, Terabyte,' Lexi said. 'We're onto it.'

SCENE 18

Thursday 10th April, Early evening

'Chapulines?' Troy turned up his nose. 'What are they?'

'Grasshoppers toasted with garlic and lime. Want to try?'

'Er … No, thanks. I'll stick with sausages.'

'Any scorpions in them?' Lexi asked with a grin.

'It's a mystery. No one's quite sure what they're made of. Pork, offal, horse?'

'You don't even know what you're eating!'

'I know they taste nice, especially when they're swimming in brown sauce.'

Lexi tried to imitate her new partner. 'Weird.'

Under a darkening sky, she was still licking her dessert – an ant lollipop – when they arrived at the homeless centre.

The building was at the edge of Foreditch's commercial hub, next to the temple, in the grounds of the cemetery. It had probably once belonged to the temple but now it was dedicated to helping the displaced. The manager was not much older than Troy and Lexi. She introduced herself as Skye and she showed them around, pushing open doors so they could see inside every part.

'We provide hot meals and drinks,' she said in the main room, which was a modest self-service canteen and seating area. 'Our most important function.' She opened another door on a small dormitory. 'And a few beds. On a first-come, first-served basis. Never enough in winter but okay at this time of year.' She flung back another door, revealing an office. 'My bit of space for getting things organized. It's open, though. No secrets here.' There were a couple of phones and three desktop computers. A homeless woman was seated at one of them. 'They can go online here, if they want. I encourage it.'

'Why?'

Skye sniffed. 'A connection to the rest of the world. Makes them feel part of the community. Less alone.'

'Have you come across The Solitude Network?' Troy asked.

'Sure. I recommend it. Very comforting. Nothing wrong with that, is there?'

'I'm just not sure it's as safe as it looks. But you're not to know that.' Troy nodded towards Lexi's life-logger. 'We want to show you a picture of someone. I warn you, it's not very pleasant because he's dead, I'm afraid. But I want to know if you recognize him.'

Skye peered at the cleaned-up image of L4G#1, screwed up her face and sighed. 'Jerome Eleven. Think so anyway. Pretty sure.'

'One of your clients?'

Skye nodded. 'A regular. Then he stopped.' She turned away momentarily, obviously upset.

'Weren't you suspicious?'

'No. It's normal in this game. People come in a lot and then they don't. Remember, they're drifters.'

'Did he use The Solitude Network?'

'Think so. Yes.'

'When did you last see him?'

Skye shrugged. 'Weeks ago.'

Taken aback, Troy glanced at Lexi. The decomposition of the body wasn't consistent with death that long ago. 'Are you sure it was weeks?'

'Couldn't put my finger on a date.'

'But weeks rather than days?'

'Definitely.'

'Did he tell you anything about his online browsing?'

'I don't ask. It's private.'

'Before he left, did he tell you what he intended to do?'

'No.'

Disappointed, Troy switched his attention to the heart from L4G#4. 'Can you think of an outer – man or woman – who used The Solitude Network near the end of last month and then didn't come back?'

Skye frowned. 'That's not enough to go on. Maybe, but … I wouldn't be able to suggest any names.'

Afterwards, Lexi sat beside Troy on a bench in the cemetery as overhead threatening clouds thickened. In the gloom, she looked at her partner and said, 'We don't know anything about the outer heart, but we've got names for all the bodies now. That'll make you a happy major.'

Troy's face remained creased. 'Happier, but south of happy.'

'I know what's bothering you. The timing doesn't add up, does it? Samaritan 999 got kicked off The Solitude Network around the time Olga died. The last week of March. I'm convinced Jerome Eleven was murdered on 4th April, so how did Samaritan 999 arrange to meet him?'

'Exactly. Even if Samaritan 999 logged on under a different username, Jerome was drifting, probably nowhere near a computer.'

'Maggots aren't like humans. They don't lie. Jerome died last Friday.'

Suddenly, Troy's face lit up. 'Unless ... Yes. It's obvious.'

'Don't tell me. He fixed up a meeting with Samaritan 999 weeks ago. They got together a few times. Days, weeks went by before Samaritan 999 smacked him on the back of the head and stole his organs.'

'No. That wasn't what I was going to say. They had their meeting ages ago and that's when Jerome disappeared.'

'But ... '

'Suspended animation.'

'What?'

'Any hospital or clinic can chill a patient. They slow the body chemistry right down,' Troy said.

'Cryonics. He'd be as good as dead but the organs would be preserved, ready for use.'

'That's a tidy explanation,' Lexi admitted. 'But I'm puzzled. Why didn't I think of it?'

'Why should you?'

'Because he's an outer like me and outers have been known to hibernate – in a way.'

'Really?'

'It's not an everyday event. It's halfway between myth and fact. Some outers have dropped their heart rates to ten or fifteen beats a minute in life-threatening situations. It helps them to survive critical injuries or illnesses. Gives doctors more time to sort out a treatment, like going into slow motion. Something you majors can't do.'

Troy nodded. 'Some rogue clinic kept him on ice till they harvested what they wanted. Then they disposed of his body last Friday. It all fits.'

'Maybe that's why we're drawing a blank on the outer heart. L4G#4 could have been put in hibernation ages ago.'

'True.'

Lexi turned towards him and said, 'Pretty good reasoning for someone who's not clever.'

Troy smiled. 'Once a heart, lungs, kidney or whatever are removed from a body, how long do they last? I'm not clever enough to know.'

'They start going downhill straightaway so it's best to operate as soon as possible. I think they're still okay after a few hours in a chiller. That's what Gianna Humble said. Something about chilling an organ till the recipient's ready. I'll do some research and firm it up.'

Almost at once, Troy jolted upright.

'What … ?'

Jumping to his feet and pointing at a figure heading for the homeless centre through the increasing darkness, Troy exclaimed, 'That's Huw!'

As soon as the two detectives began to move towards him, Huw spotted them, turned and ran in the opposite direction, making for a gate from the cemetery onto a riverside path. A rucksack bounced up and down on his back.

Within seconds, Lexi was strides ahead of Troy and hail began to pelt them. The sudden storm distorted Troy's vision and the vicious balls of ice stung his skin. He screwed up his face so the hail had less chance of hitting his eyes.

At the gate, Huw and Lexi had turned left towards the commercial heart of Foreditch. Countless hailstones hurled themselves at the river, rippling the surface so the water appeared to be boiling. On the other side, the frozen rain clattered loudly against an approaching train that was reducing its speed as it neared the station.

Lexi's burst of speed had not yet faded. Troy didn't see much point in simply following her. He needed a different tactic. Above the storm, he yelled, 'Immediate backup needed for Lexi Iona Four. Trace her life-logger. Can't be far from Foreditch Crime Central.' He dashed towards a bridge that spanned both the river and the railway. On the other side, he vaulted over the fence and sprinted up a short grassy slope onto the stones beside the track. Taking a deep breath, he ran alongside the train. When the last carriage came past, he leapt between the rails and accelerated. Gritting his teeth, he surged forward as fast as he was able and threw himself at the back of the coach. He grabbed a cold metal bar with both arms and his feet found the metal plate. There, he clung on tightly. Relieved. He'd acted on impulse – a dangerous impulse that might have got him injured or killed – but he was elated as well.

The train continued to brake but, even so, Troy overtook two people scampering through the hailstorm on the far river bank. As far as Troy could see, Lexi was lagging further behind Huw. As an outer, she was probably running out of steam. Neither of them noticed Troy on his unconventional and perilous perch.

When the train passed over the river and slowed to walking pace, Troy jumped off and scrambled onto the river bank. There, behind the entertainment complex, he waited. The path had turned white with small frozen spheres. The storm had eased a little but hail still bounced off his head and shoulders. The sky remained dark as nightfall loomed.

Within seconds, Huw saw Troy ahead and skidded to a halt. Puzzled, he stood still, uncertain. Then he turned slowly round, clearly wondering who he'd prefer to tackle – Troy or an exhausted Lexi.

'I'm tired,' Lexi called out as she drew close to him, 'but I still don't think you want to take me on. You might be surprised who comes off worse.'

On cue, two police officers from Foreditch Crime Central raced onto the path and positioned themselves behind her.

Huw glanced at the river and Troy realized that, just for an instant, he was thinking about making his escape by diving into the water and swimming. With a rail bridge nearby and four people against him, though, he must have decided that the attempt would fail. He would also have known that his every move would be captured by life-loggers.

Huw's shoulders sagged. He was trapped. Game over.

A train sauntered out of town as Troy walked up to him. At the same time, Troy's life-logger vibrated with an incoming message. When he saw it, Troy laughed. He held it up towards Huw and said, 'Look. Memo from the team near Langhorn Reservoir. "No sign of subject Huw. No fresh graves in the wood."'

'You thought I might be dead?'

'It's a murder scene and you disappeared,' Troy answered. 'It was one theory. But it's not holding up well right now. Another was that you're a suspect. Running away adds to that impression.'

Still panting, Lexi joined them. Immediately, she glanced down to confirm Huw's shoe size. The two officers stayed within a few paces in case they were needed.

'But … ' Flustered, Huw hesitated.

'Yes?'

'You took me by surprise, turning up here. I suppose I panicked. I haven't done anything wrong. I was just scared I made myself look guilty because I told you I was staying put, but didn't.'

'Why did you move on?' Troy asked.

'I didn't like all the … commotion in the wood. Nothing more than that. I like peace and quiet.'

'What's in your backpack?'

'All my worldly goods. And it's nowhere near full.'

'Some sharp tools?'

'A few specialist ones for carving. Not many.'

'Why come here?' Troy said.

'I told you before. I volunteer at the homeless centre.'

'Do you know a man called Jerome who used to drop in now and again?'

Huw shook his head. 'Doesn't ring a bell. No.'

'Well, here's my problem. One of our victims was here before his body turned up next to Langhorn Reservoir. Now I find out you help out at the same place and you were living a stone's throw from his grave. Your shoeprint's right there, next to it. You're the common factor.'

Huw opened his mouth to say something but failed to find the words.

Lexi said, 'You know we're going to arrest you, don't you? We can't have you running off again.' She looked at the police reinforcements and said, 'It's a charge of resisting arrest for now.'

'But,' Huw spluttered, 'I wouldn't bury someone right next to my own cabin, would I? That'd be stupid.'

Quick as a flash, Lexi replied, 'It's not just clever people who commit crimes. Stupid people do it too.'

Troy smiled. 'The reason you're not facing something more serious is because we know someone else is involved. Do you want to tell us about an accomplice?'

'I can't. I don't … '

'Where did you get the trolley?'

'Trolley? What trolley?'

Huw looked suitably surprised and bewildered.

'All right,' Troy said. 'We'll stick at resisting arrest. For one thing, I don't think you're stupid.' To the uniformed officers, he said, 'Don't forget to check his bag. I think you'll find some sharp instruments in it.'

While Troy and Lexi watched Huw being led away, the hail finally came to an end. Lexi looked at her partner and said, 'Just tell me one thing. How did you get here so quickly?'

'Technically,' he replied, 'I think it's called cheating.'

'That's not an answer.'

'A major has to preserve his mystery. Anyway, what about you? What was that bit about him coming off worse if he took you on?'

'You only met me three days ago. Nowhere near long enough to probe the vast depths of an outer.'

SCENE 19

Friday 11th April, Morning

Lexi had not wasted the night. Between bouts of meditation, she had assembled a spreadsheet that summarized their case. She pointed at the first entry and said, 'A spot of research told me L4G#1's full name is Jerome Sebastian Eleven. He went off-grid two years ago. Killed and harvested for body parts last Friday but, because of the modern invention of cryonics, he could have been snatched weeks ago. Used The Solitude Network website.'

Troy sat and watched her, admiring her crisp and unemotional assessments.

'A simple overnight DNA check using skin and hair from Olga Wylie's house proves she's L4G#2. No big shock there. Probably died around Tuesday 25th March. Body not harvested. She received a transplant instead. A huge gaffe gave her an outer's heart and a quick death. Also used The Solitude Network website. Someone in size twelve shoes broke into her house and trod the ground near the place she was buried.

'L4G#3 is Dmitri Backhouse. Died about 25th February. Possible assisted suicide arranged online via a suicide chat room. A thoroughly harvested body. Just about every usable bit taken.' Lexi paused and added, 'Note the online connection between all three.' Then she sighed. 'L4G#4's a mystery. All we've got is an outer heart. It must have been available on 25th March or thereabouts because, in a way, it became the weapon that killed Olga Wylie.' Gazing at Troy, she asked, 'Am I boring you?'

'No. I know it all, but a review's really helpful. What about the clues that're floating in mid-air?'

Lexi pointed to the right-hand side of the screen. 'That'll be the unknown cart tracks, the size twelve shoeprints and the list of people with a fishing licence for Langhorn Reservoir – no one on it related to the case yet.'

'And the evidence we'd love to find – Dmitri's and Olga's computers.'

'True. Now, suspects. Not a lot to say. Not a lot of them. Huw, the displaced wood-carver. Under arrest in Foreditch. Connected to Jerome Eleven through Foreditch Homeless Centre. Connected to all victims by living in the wood and his shoeprints near their graves. Not size twelve, though. And … ' She turned to face Troy. 'Neither of us thinks he did it, do we?'

'No. He doesn't care enough about money to make more of it by harvesting bodies.'

Lexi nodded. 'There's just a niggling doubt he knows more than he's saying, or he helped the bad guy in some way.' Focusing on the screen again, she continued, 'The Rural Retreat Transplant Clinic. Its location – and its business – makes the whole organization an obvious suspect. But no evidence whatsoever, despite camera surveillance.' She shrugged. 'And we've got vague online suspects. Samaritan 999 trawls The Solitude Network and Charon Angel's active in the suicide chat room. Perhaps picking on the vulnerable. But Charon Angel posts stuff that could be perfectly innocent and lives in Switzerland. Which isn't very convenient for committing murders in Shepford. So,' she said, 'what do you conclude, oh perceptive one?'

Troy smiled. 'I conclude we need more information, oh methodical one. But … '

'What?'

'It's still the internet trawlers I'm most interested in.'

'You're confusing gut instinct with logic and common sense. You can't kill people here if you're in Switzerland.'

'True. But that begs a question.'

'Does it?'

Troy nodded. 'How do we know for sure Charon Angel's in Switzerland?'

'Terabyte found out online.'

'Do you believe everything it says online? I don't think so.'

'The site administrator – Sergio Treize – said so as well.'

'Do you always believe witnesses – and the data they've been given by a suspect?'

'No, but it's a good bet the size twelves don't fit her,' Lexi replied.

'That begs another question.'

'Oh?'

'How do we know Charon Angel's female?'

'Because Terabyte found out her real name's Sharon.'

'More online information,' Troy observed. 'Not exactly proof.'

'So, where do you go from here?'

Troy sighed. 'I'm thinking about it.'

Distracted by her life-logger, Lexi read the latest messages with a broad grin on her face. 'You know you wanted more information? Well ... '

'What have you got?'

'The results on Olga Wylie,' Lexi replied. 'Something and nothing. First, the nothing. There's no record of travel before she disappeared. Maybe she turned up and bought a train ticket with cash. Or the underground clinic is within walking distance.'

'Or the clinic sent a car for her.'

'Here's the something,' said Lexi. She transmitted a photograph to the screen so Troy could see the rich blue gemstone. 'Found at Olga Wylie's place. It's a sapphire and the team found nothing that matched it among Olga's jewellery, so it could have come from the intruder. It was hidden in the carpet pile near her desk.'

The round sapphire had been photographed alongside a ruler, showing that it was barely two millimetres in diameter.

'It was clean,' Lexi told him. 'No DNA. The sort of stone that fits into a brooch or a ring. Part of a decoration.'

'Well,' Troy said. 'You're right. It's something. Can your wizard forensics give it some welly?'

'Pardon?'

'Can you do any fancy analysis on it?'

'Oh, yes. There's always something. Microspectrometry in this case, I should think. Different gems absorb and reflect light at different wavelengths. That's why the colour varies. It's all down to charged iron particles in each bit of sapphire.'

'So, you can tell if this stone matches another one in the same piece of jewellery?'

'I can map the colours – in the visible and ultraviolet parts of the spectrum – and find out if they're much the same. If they are, hey presto, they'll have the same source.'

'All we need is an item of jewellery with a hole instead of one of its sapphires, then.'

'Yeah. And the person who's wearing it.' For the benefit of her life-logger, she said, 'I'll get the lab to do the spectrometry.'

'Would it be expensive, this sapphire? It's tiny but I don't know anything about jewellery.'

'Sapphire's pricey, but one that size … Not cheap, but it wouldn't ruin you.'

'Any other finds?' Troy asked.

'No, but Kofi Seven wants to see us in Pathology.'

SCENE 20

Friday 11th April, Mid-morning

Kofi stood back from the female body on the plinth and gave the small electric saw to his assistant. 'You do it. Standard access to her brain, please. I need to talk to these two. It won't take long.'

Shivering at the whine of the rotating blade and then the dreadful grinding noise, Troy didn't look back to watch the deputy's work. He left the room with Lexi and the lanky pathologist.

In the corridor, Kofi ran a hand over his hairless head. 'I got a specialist to run more extensive tests on the DNA from the outer's heart. L4G#4. As you'll know, it's usually about matching one DNA profile with another in a database. Does profile A match B? If so, A is B – or at least an identical twin. But with time and care, these days you can build up a picture from DNA. You can deduce gender, hair and eye colour and estimate height and weight. It's never perfect but it's better than nothing at all.'

'What can you tell us about L4G#4?' Lexi asked eagerly.

'Gender, female. Almost certain. Brown eyes, ninety-four per cent sure. Blonde hair, but not so sure. Sixty-seven per cent likely, I'm told. Height somewhere between you and me. Average weight for an outer. Quite slender.'

'Odds on the height and weight?' Lexi prompted.

'Slightly better than guesswork. Now,' Kofi said, 'if you don't mind, I've got a brain to remove, slice and examine.'

'Thanks,' Troy said.

Lexi nodded her appreciation. Once Kofi had gone back into the cold laboratory, she said to her partner, 'You did ask for more information. That god of yours is smiling on you today.'

SCENE 21

Monday 7th April, Early afternoon

Troy and Lexi had agreed to share the workload. Troy tried to find out if a woman matching the description of L4G#4 had died recently in dubious circumstances. Lexi trawled through databases of missing persons.

'How's it going?' Troy asked her.

'Not easy. She could have been abducted ages ago and kept on ice. But I've got one candidate. I'm sending a crime scene officer to get a sample of her DNA from where she used to live. I'll see if it matches L4G#4's heart.' She swallowed a crispy-fried beetle and washed it down with white wine. 'How about you?'

'Waiting. I've put out a request to hospitals for a female outer – brown eyes, blonde hair, average build and a healthy heart – who suffered a suspicious death in the last week of March. And I put in a bit about anything weird happening after death. Like a scar appearing on her chest. I sent it to all mortuaries, undertakers and crematoria, just in case.'

Lexi grinned mischievously. 'Not to temples, though.'

Troy knew his partner was baiting him. 'Somehow, I don't think an outer would opt for a temple burial. But God made all creatures great and small. That includes outers, even if you won't admit it.'

'Hey. Don't inflict your god on us,' Lexi said. 'There's no need to conjure up the supernatural to explain life. That's what science does. It explains everything – including the evolution of both human races.'

'Science is the brick wall you build against belief in God. Scientific explanations have got nothing to do with it.' He took a drink of blueberry juice.

'All right,' Lexi said, as if she were accepting a challenge. 'If your god made his presence felt right now in this room – officially and undeniably recorded on life-logger – you wouldn't be happy, would you? Proof that God exists does away with your need for faith.'

'I wouldn't be as unhappy as you,' Troy replied with a smirk.

Lexi laughed. 'True. It'd be a bit embarrassing from my point of view. I'll give you that. But, let's face it, it's not going to happen. We can both carry on being happy. I say there's no such thing as an invisible overlord and you keep the faith.' Plainly, she couldn't resist a final dig because she added, 'Even though it's irrational.'

'Maybe it is a bit crazy but, with all the bad stuff we see in this job, it's helpful. It reassures me.' Checking his life-logger, Troy frowned. 'What do you make of this? It's ... um ... a hall of rest, they call it. A place to keep coffins – of majors or outers – before burial or cremation. Usually just overnight.'

'A posh mortuary, then?'

'I guess. It's never locked up in case families want to spend time with ... Anyway, they've had a few hints that someone's been up to no good now and again. Scratched coffins and the like. Not serious vandalism.'

'Are these coffins closed? Are the lids fixed down?'

Troy read the details from his life-logger. 'As a general rule, majors' coffins are left open for families and friends who want to say their goodbyes. Outers' are usually sealed, ready for cremation.'

'So,' Lexi said, suddenly interested, 'if I was after body parts, it'd be simple to take stuff from majors, but it's almost certainly going to be noticed. If I wanted parts from an outer, I'd just need a lever to force open a coffin, take what I want, reseal, and, hey presto, no one would know a thing about it.'

'Exactly. You might leave a scratch or two on the coffin. Nothing more.'

Lexi threw the last fried beetle into her mouth, crunched it up, and finished the wine. 'Let's get going. Where is this place anyway?'

'Hurlstone. We're off to the seaside.'

SCENE 22

Friday 11th April, Evening

They stood together on top of the cliff and, as the sun dipped towards the horizon, watched the sea. The hall of rest behind them, the scene was suitably peaceful. The breeze coming off the sea was light and cool. Miniature waves caressed the rocky beach below, hardly making a noise, barely jostling the stones and pebbles.

'Crumbly cliffs,' Lexi said. 'Hurlstone's well known for fossils. Somewhere down there – in a cave – archaeologists found evidence of our common ancestor, *Homo erectus*. Before we split into two species six hundred thousand years ago. They even managed to get some DNA out of the bones.'

'Makes me wonder,' Troy replied. 'If we find out who owned the outer heart – and she's been cremated – how do we prove it? Where do we get her DNA from?'

'That's my job,' Lexi said. 'I'll think of something. If archaeologists can get it out of a dried-up bone that's thousands of years old, I'll get some for L4G#4.' She turned her back on the cliff top and said, 'Let's go and see.'

The hall of rest was serene, not macabre and analytical like the pathology laboratory. Speaking in a hush, the supervisor had a similar air of calm about him. 'I know everyone respects what we do here,' he said. 'I'd never expect any … trouble. It's unthinkable really. I can't imagine why anyone would … ' He ran out of words.

'Sadly, we can,' said Troy. 'Someone might want to break in because there's an illegal trade in body parts.'

Spike Pennyworth stared at him. 'Do you mean … ?'

Troy nodded. 'A good heart's valuable, especially to a transplant patient who doesn't want to wait in the normal hospital queue.'

'But that's … ' Spike seemed to have difficulty in

finishing many of his sentences. Even so, his quiet outrage was plain.

'We're trying to find out if one of your disturbed coffins belonged to a female outer.' Troy was about to give his vague description of L4G#4 when Lexi stepped in.

'She'd be a bit like me. Taller perhaps, but the same brown eyes and blonde hair – probably.'

'Same age?'

'We don't know about age,' Troy told him. 'But her heart would have been in good condition when she died.'

'When was this?' he asked.

'Tuesday 25th March, or maybe the day before,' Lexi said. 'Once someone's dead, there's only a few hours to use the heart. It'd have to be removed, put in preserving fluid and chilled quite quickly.' Clearly, she had done some extra research.

'Spare me the details,' Spike said with a grimace. 'Let me check my diary.'

His records were entirely on paper. He flicked backwards through the large pages until he came to a halt on one particular entry. It described a client who had arrived on the evening of 24th March and rested overnight before cremation on the 25th. He tapped the page and the photographs. 'Tiffany Clara

One, according to some ID in her pocket. She was a bit of a mystery but she matches your description. She wasn't visited by anyone. She was cremated – with her possessions – the next day.'

Judging by the photograph of her deathly pale face, Tiffany One was in her twenties. While Lexi scanned the page into her life-logger, Troy asked, 'Cause of death?'

The supervisor sighed. 'A fall. Down the cliff.'

'She fell over the cliff? An accident?'

'It could have been an accident, but … '

'What?'

'It wasn't. There's a fence up to stop … You haven't heard Hurlstone's claim to fame, have you?'

Troy frowned. 'Fossils?'

'I wish that was all it was,' Spike replied. 'No. A few people who decide to end it all come here and … '

'They jump off the cliff?'

He nodded, apparently unable to confirm it in words.

'Does it happen a lot?'

'Mercifully, no.'

'How often?'

'There's usually one or two each year. Still enough to get us a reputation.'

'Where exactly does this happen?' Lexi asked.

'It's about a kilometre – to the south.' Spike waved in the general direction. 'There's a big overhang. Quite dangerous. They've put up a fence to try to stop people, make them think again, but … '

Lexi examined the photograph of Tiffany One's meagre possessions and then said, 'Let's go and take a look, before we lose daylight altogether.'

'Okay,' Troy agreed. 'But we'll be back,' he said to Spike. 'If Hurlstone's got a reputation, this place would appeal to someone after body parts for the black market. I want Lexi to put a camera in here.'

'I don't like the idea of spying on grieving … '

'We won't. We'll monitor the cameras, spying on intruders, not people who've lost a friend or family member.'

'Do I have a choice?'

'Not really,' Troy answered. 'But you should be pleased. You'll want to get this sorted out as much as we do. A tiny camera no one will notice is the quickest way. Then you'll be back to normal.'

'The sun's going down,' Lexi reminded her partner.

'Back soon,' he said to the troubled supervisor.

SCENE 23

Friday 11th April, Sundown

The remains of the sun sent a yellow beam across the sea from the horizon. It was just enough light for Troy and Lexi. Near the edge of the cliff, there were several notices giving details of organizations that could offer advice and help. There was also a wire fence and a warning notice. A long way below, there was nothing but vicious jagged rocks.

Troy checked out the fence. 'That's not going to stop anyone determined,' he said.

'You're right,' Lexi replied, stepping back and taking a short run at it. 'I'm going over.'

'You're what?'

'Going over the fence.'

'Careful.'

'I didn't know you cared.' Sprinting past him, she flew over the fence in one athletic leap.

'Why are you … ?'

Heading for the overhang, she pointed to a spot one stride away from the sheer drop. 'Collecting evidence,' she said, quickly putting on latex gloves. 'See that bit of blue material on the gorse? If I'm not mistaken, it matches Tiffany One's coat in the photographs.'

'That's thin ice you're skating on,' Troy called after her. 'Watch out. Crumbly cliffs, remember.'

She stepped carefully towards the bush, the piece of fabric and the cliff. 'One day, I'll make an interesting fossil,' she said as she peered over the unnerving rock face. She took a breath of sea breeze, plucked the material from the prickly gorse and immediately made for the safety of the cliff-top path. 'But not yet.' She clambered back over the fence and held out the small piece of fabric. 'Hard to tell in this light but I'll check the colour with the photo. If there's a flake of skin, this is a shortcut to her DNA. Then we don't have to find where she lived.'

SCENE 24

Saturday 12th April, Morning

'That woman I found on the missing persons' list,' Lexi announced, 'isn't L4G#4. Her DNA profile is nothing like.'

'What about Tiffany One?' Troy asked, unwrapping a sturdy chunk of black pudding.

Lexi sat back and closed her eyes, just about to enter another period of meditation. 'Waiting,' she murmured. 'Relax. Patience required.'

Twelve minutes later, her life-logger vibrated and she stirred slowly.

Troy called out, 'Rise and shine.'

Refreshed, Lexi sniffed. 'What is that?' She looked at the remains of Troy's breakfast and let out a groan. 'Yuck.'

'Black pudding. Shiveringly good.'

'What's in it?' she asked. 'Smells revolting.'

'It's a sausage made of pigs' blood, onions and oatmeal. Or something like that.'

'A sausage made of blood? Disgusting.'

'At least it doesn't crawl around like your insect food. It's not a baked spider or whatever.'

'Spiders and scorpions aren't insects. They're arachnids.'

'All right. Let's call them bugs, then.'

'Or invertebrates,' she replied, reaching for her life-logger, 'but that would include some major favourites – like prawns. Not as tasty as a bowl of caramelized mealworms.' She read from the screen and smiled. 'Hey presto. The DNA on the blue material is a pretty good match with L4G#4. We may only have her heart, but I think we've got her name. Tiffany Clara One.' Straightaway, she began to update her spreadsheet. 'One homeless man, one transplant error and two suicides. That's probably one real suicide and one that the victim definitely didn't perform himself.'

'That's called murder. And it happened to both

Dmitri Backhouse and Jerome Eleven. We've got a whole load of other charges as well. Unlawful killing in the case of Olga Wylie, burglary at her house, probable abduction of Jerome, mutilation of bodies for sure, prevention of proper burial or cremation of three of them. I bet we'd think of some more if we put our minds to it.'

'I doubt they're the only victims,' Lexi said. 'When we get the bad guy and the clinic, I reckon there'll be lots more we don't know about yet. Lots more offences. Your first case is going to set some sort of record.'

'If we crack it.'

'You're with me, remember,' Lexi replied. 'We'll crack it.'

'We've got plenty on the victims. But the culprit? That's a dead horse I've been flogging. Going nowhere.'

Lexi smiled. 'Things don't look good when your best suspect's not even in the right country.'

'But … '

'Yeah. I know. We don't have total proof she's … '

Troy got to his feet. 'I'm going to take a look at that interview with Sergio Treize.'

'Why? What's it going to tell you?'

'Maybe nothing, but you never know. There's something I want to check out.'

Using a giant screen at maximum resolution, Troy put the video recording on fast-forward until he got to the part where he suggested that Charon Angel could be scouting for body parts. Then he ran the interview at normal speed.

There was a convincing expression of shock on Sergio's face as he exclaimed, 'What?'

Out of camera-shot, Troy's detached voice said, 'For medical transplants.'

Sergio replied, 'I find that hard to believe.' Then he turned his head to the side and stroked his chin for a few seconds.

'That's it!' Troy cried. He stopped the clip and ran it backwards in slow motion until he reached the frame he wanted. There, he froze the action. Stepping up to the screen, he said, 'Look at his wrist.'

Lexi shrugged. 'It's a watch. A traditional Swiss one.'

'I'll zoom in on it. See? Can you make it out? What time does it say?'

'Er ... A quarter past one or thereabouts.'

Troy nodded. Jabbing his finger towards the digital clock in the corner of the large monitor, he said, 'Thirteen sixteen.'

For a moment, Lexi was silent but then she also jumped up. 'The same time zone as us. Sergio Treize wasn't in Switzerland! He's local.' She hesitated again before grabbing her mobile. 'I'll call Terabyte.'

Troy scrutinized more images from the video call while Lexi reminded Terabyte about the interview with Sergio Treize. Then she asked, 'Did the call definitely come from Switzerland?'

She put his response on loudspeaker.

'Yes.'

'Are you sure?'

'Absolutely. I traced it and it was definitely Swiss. But ... '

'What?'

'Well, I suppose ... ' Terabyte went quiet for a moment. 'It's possible Switzerland wasn't the source. If someone was being devious – really devious – they could've been anywhere in the world and relayed it through Switzerland. You'd need a lot of insider knowledge.'

'The sort of knowledge a website administrator might have?'

'I guess.'

'Thanks, Terabyte.' She put her phone down and concentrated on the screen again. 'You had a feeling he wasn't in Switzerland, didn't you?' she said to Troy. 'You were right. But, thinking about it, this is all about Sergio Treize. What's it got to do with Charon Angel?'

'Look at his sweatshirt. The image on it.'

'Yeah. I think it's … Let me check.' Lexi tapped some keys on her computer, running image recognition software. 'Yes, it's a band sweatshirt. The group's called Kaktus Changer – death metal from Iceland.'

'And, according to Terabyte, what had Charon – Sharon Angie – been buying?'

'Icelandic music.'

Troy nodded. 'Exactly.'

'There was something else,' said Lexi. 'She bought car parts online and she lives in a place called Wengen. But, listen to this.' She read from some tourist information on the Swiss village. 'It has a tranquil atmosphere because it is a rare example of a European resort that is free of cars.' She looked at her partner and said, 'Why buy car parts when no one's got a car? Don't tell me. You think Sergio Treize, Charon Angel and Sharon Angie are all the same person – and they don't live anywhere near Wengen.'

'That's not all. I reckon he's Samaritan 999 as well. All these identities are a front – to hide his dodgy activities.' Adjusting the onscreen display so it showed the close-up of Sergio's hand again, Troy said, 'Check out his middle finger.'

Lexi squinted at the image. 'Can't you sharpen it up a bit?'

'No. It's at its limit. Any closer and all you'll get are pixels.'

She sighed. 'Well, there's a slight mark. It runs round the whole finger, I think.'

'And the skin colour's a bit lighter.'

'So,' Lexi deduced, 'he normally wears a ring – which stops the sun tanning him just there. He's not wearing it now, though.'

'Why not?'

'How should I know?' said Lexi.

'I don't either. But if it had sapphires in it and one of the stones dropped out ... '

'I was with you all the way there – till you started daydreaming. Are you going to claim you can tell his shoe size by looking at his hands?'

'No. But,' Troy said with a wry expression, 'that sweatshirt would go really nicely with Adibok trainers.'

Lexi laughed.

'We need Terabyte again,' Troy said. 'Can you talk nicely to him? Maybe he can trace where Sergio Treize really is if I keep him on a video call for long enough.'

Half an hour later, Troy settled himself in front of his computer. On his left, Terabyte was seated at a linked workstation. Lexi was on the other side. Both of them were out of range of the camera. 'Okay?' he asked.

'I'm networked,' Terabyte told him. 'Ready when you are.'

Lexi nodded. She intended to listen for background noises and study the images for any hints of location.

'Okay. Let's push this boat out.'

Lexi looked across at Terabyte, raised her eyebrows and shrugged. She took the headphones from around her neck and positioned them over her head and onto her ears.

Troy soon established a connection to his main suspect. This time, Sergio was wearing a different sweatshirt. Plain and white, it matched his spectacles. From somewhere, light reflected from his smoothly shaved head.

'Sorry to bother you again,' Troy began. 'I just wanted to ask if you've been monitoring Charon Angel, like we agreed.'

'I don't remember an agreement but, yes, as a favour, I've checked her out now and again. All perfectly innocent.' He leaned to one side, apparently scrolling down a list. 'Here's an example. She was posting stuff on Wednesday to someone who's serious about suicide. "If you go ahead, your absence will change the way things are supposed to be. It's a shame to deny the world your contribution." No one's going to say that's urging a visitor to die, are they?'

'No. That's ... good. Helpful. I'm still worried about your site, though.'

'Oh?'

'It's a place where vulnerable people meet. Virtually meet. Maybe they don't have the strength or the nerve or whatever you need to pull the plug alone but, when they get together, maybe they pluck up enough courage from each other.' Troy noticed a flicker of annoyance in Sergio's face. That suited him. 'Why did you set the site up in the first place?'

'To get people together so they could pluck up the courage to live.'

'But not all of them do.' Troy was trying to provoke Sergio enough to keep him talking – justifying his chat room – but not anger him so much that he terminated the connection. 'Some of your visitors are exchanging how-to-die information.'

'For a determined few, it's the only way forward. My site eases their passage.'

'It's a fine line between easing and encouraging.'

His head twitched. 'Look. I believe we all have the

right to die. The law in your country is stupid. It tells you you're responsible for your body and actions, if you're over ten and sane. So, if you do something illegal, you get punished. Right. Got that. I'm responsible for my body and what I do with it. Surely that means, if I get really ill and nothing will fix me, I can choose to bow out with a bit of dignity when the time's right. I can choose assisted death. After all, it's my body, my life, my responsibility. Right? Wrong, says the law. You're not responsible for your body any more. The law is.'

Troy was pleased to have tempted him into a lengthy passionate lecture. 'It's not against the law to kill yourself.'

'No. But you can't get anyone to help. You can't legally take that decision. See what I'm getting at? The law's sending out a mixed message. In your country anyway. I'm responsible for my actions until I'm desperately ill and suffering. Then I'm not responsible. Most of us get help coming into this world. Where's the help when we choose to leave it? What's so bad about opting for assisted dying?'

'Because there's always a reason for living. There's always hope. But, even if I agreed with you, it's still illegal.'

'It's different over here. I'm glad your law doesn't

apply to me. When I'm past it and life has lost its meaning, when it's just useless existence and a drain on everyone else,' Sergio said, 'I'll slip away peacefully with help and humanity.'

Out of the corner of his eye, Troy saw Terabyte fling his hair over his shoulder and mutter to himself. He then sat upright and, plainly frustrated, shook his head. Troy knew he had failed. Troy's strategy had not worked. He said to Sergio, 'That's your choice, I guess. Nothing I can do about it from here. Thanks for your time.' He ended the call.

Lexi stripped off her headphones and, along with Troy, gazed at Terabyte.

'The signal's pinging all over the place, from country to country, satellite to satellite. If I sat here online for a week, I'd still probably not pin it down. Very nice piece of work. All I can say is, it came here from Switzerland. Before that ... Who knows?'

'Thanks for trying.' Troy faced his partner and asked, 'Did you pick up anything?'

'There was a distant scream. Not a human one. Pretty sure it was a seagull. That's your lot.'

Troy exhaled. 'I'm not sure that puts him near the coast. Don't seagulls come inland quite a bit?'

'I've seen a few around here,' said Lexi, 'but it's asking a lot for them to reach Switzerland.'

'This case isn't hurtling towards a conclusion, is it?'

Lexi thought about it for a while and then said, 'There is another way ... But it won't be much fun.'

'What's that?'

'Well,' Lexi replied, 'he didn't see me in either call. He doesn't know what I look like. So ... '

'Oh, no,' Troy muttered.

'What?'

'Are you thinking the same as me?'

'No idea. But if an extremely healthy outer girl – about sixteen, all organs functioning beautifully – jumped off Hurlstone cliff, our bad guy might not be able to resist a raid.'

Troy nodded slowly. 'Are you really volunteering to pose as a dead body? You could be trapped in a coffin for hours.'

'The lid wouldn't have to be nailed down – and I could be wired so I could speak to you.'

'I'm glad *you* made the suggestion. I was thinking the same, but I sure wasn't going to ask you to stay in a coffin all night in case he turns up.'

'Lying down and keeping still doesn't sound like a tough assignment. I'd meditate while you monitor the spy camera. You give me a wake-up call if he puts in an appearance. That's quite important, Troy. I don't want to spend the rest of my life without a heart.'

'I won't let you down.' Troy turned towards Terabyte. 'Can you get the story out on the media and internet? Everywhere you can think of. "Hurlstone cliff claims the life of second girl this year. An unknown outer, sixteen years old, leapt to her death this evening." That sort of thing. Make sure you mention the Hurlstone hall of rest.'

'No problem.'

'Put seven o'clock in the report,' Lexi suggested. 'Then he's got five hours if he wants my lungs or heart. After that decay will make them useless. Hey presto. All over by midnight.'

'What if he wants liver or kidneys?' Troy asked.

'Then I've got a longer wait. Eight to fifteen hours. Might be a good idea to shut me in with some cricket tortillas, preferably topped with radish and orange. And run a tube from the nearest beer barrel.'

SCENE 25

Saturday 12th April, Night

In a white funeral robe, Lexi walked right around her coffin and sighed. 'It's small, isn't it?'

'It's the biggest they've got,' Troy said, 'but, no, you're not going to have a lot of room.'

'No chance of inviting a few friends round.'

'Are you sure ... ?'

'Yes.'

'We could do it with an empty coffin. If he comes in and pulls back the lid ... Maybe that's enough.'

'I'm not sure – and he might escape. If he attacks a dead body – me – on camera, we get proof and I'll be so angry, he won't stand a chance of getting away. That's a watertight case.'

'Unlike the coffin,' Troy said with a smile.

'What?'

'The coffin's not watertight – or airtight. I made sure of that when I asked for it.'

'Very reassuring.'

At seven thirty, Terabyte announced in their earpieces that the story about Lexi's tragic leap half an hour earlier had gone live.

'Okay?' Troy asked.

'I suppose,' she said.

'There's no great hurry. Sergio's got to pick up the story, decide if he wants any of your organs and then get here.'

Outside, a seagull screeched loudly.

'I think I'd better take up my position. Is my earpiece showing?'

'No. You're fine.'

The hall of rest was illuminated dimly by lights sunk into the ceiling. The coffin had been placed on a plinth about fifty centimetres off the ground. Lexi put a small torch inside, roughly where her waist would be. To steady herself as she clambered in, she gripped Troy's shoulder. Strangely, Troy felt flattered that she trusted him. Before the end of the night, she would have to rely on him much more. She wouldn't have agreed to be the lure, Troy thought, if she didn't have complete confidence in him.

Troy moved to the foot of the coffin and took hold of the lid. Before he pushed it forward and over her body, he said, 'All right?'

She adjusted her funeral gown and nodded. 'Do it.'

The lid rumbled over her, cutting her off from the real world.

There was a hidden microphone sewn into the inside of her robe. Her voice was a whisper in Troy's earpiece but it was clear. 'Can you see the light from my torch out there?'

'No. It's okay if you want it on.' He walked out of the main hall and went into the small annex. There, he spoke quietly into the microphone attached to his sweatshirt. 'Can you still hear me?'

'No.'

'Great. A dead body with a sense of humour.'

'You must be hoping we've wrapped it up by midnight, mustn't you?'

'Well … '

'Sunday's your day for skiving off to a temple.'

'Just this once, I imagine God'll forgive me if I'm still ridding the world of bad guys.'

The two spy cameras were working fine. One was trained on the entrance to the hall of rest. The other focused on the only coffin in the room. Troy had arranged with Spike Pennyworth that there would not be any corpses and none would be allowed to arrive in the night. The whole place was spookily quiet.

After half an hour, concerned for his partner, Troy checked, 'Are you okay?'

'This lying down lark isn't as easy as I thought. It's hard to relax. Even with my eyes closed and the torch off, I can tell the lid's a few centimetres from my nose. I guess this is what claustrophobia feels like. Pipe me some music, Troy. Maybe that'll help.'

'What sort?'

'Anything apart from death metal. That wouldn't be funny. There's a music app on my computer. Set it to play on random.'

Troy sat and waited, his heart thumping. Despite the cool stillness, he would not fall asleep. His eyes darted from one screen to the other. First the coffin that held his partner and then the doorway. But nothing moved. Nothing stirred at all. Not a sound.

He couldn't imagine how awful it was for Lexi. She was pretending to be dead, confined to a horribly small space, waiting for a serial killer. She had her partner as a lookout but no other backup. If they'd ringed the place with police officers, the bad guy might well have spotted the trap and refused to take the bait.

At eight thirty, Troy faded the stream of music. 'Still with me?'

'Yes. The music helps. Are you still awake?'

'No.'

'Very funny,' she whispered.

'Just getting my own back.'

'Any action yet?'

'Not a sausage.'

'You're obsessed with them,' Lexi said. 'You're not eating one now, are you?'

'No. I'm concentrating.'

'Good to hear that.'

'Tell me straightaway if you want out,' said Troy. 'Remember the empty coffin option.'

'I'm okay.'

'Here's your music again.'

Ten minutes later, Troy turned down the music volume and whispered into the microphone. 'Something's just struck me. If he opens your coffin, won't the warmth of your body give it away?'

'Dead bodies stay warm for about eight hours. They go stiff after three or thereabouts. It's breathing I'm bothered about. That's something corpses just don't do. I'm trying to calm down my metabolism. And slow my heartbeat. I can do it. It's not a myth and I'm in a sort of life-threatening situation. It's just super-meditation. Super-relaxation – or mini-hibernation.'

'Don't overdo it,' Troy said. 'You'll have to act quickly if he turns up. Do you still want me to talk to you every half hour?'

'Yes. It tells me you're awake.'

Troy chuckled. 'So, it's you checking up on me?'

'Too right.'

'Not the other way round?'

'Huh,' was her only reply.

Troy took a deep breath. His mood kept changing. Sometimes, the atmosphere seemed so serene that he could never imagine anything bad happening. At other times, the dark and the stillness were so creepy that he could imagine all too easily that something terrible was bound to take place at any moment. He felt unsettled and tense. And he was far from certain that they were doing the right thing.

At nine o'clock, Lexi didn't say much at all. She could have been half asleep. She was probably deep in meditation. If she had been a major, Troy would have called it a spiritual state. At nine thirty, her words were slow and slurred. At ten o'clock, she seemed less groggy. She was both agitated and bored.

At ten thirteen, the door into the hall of rest began to open slowly.

Immediately, Troy's heart thudded alarmingly in his chest. He jumped up and bent over the monitor. 'Lexi,' he said in an urgent hush. 'Can you hear me?'

'Yes.'

'Don't say anything else, just listen to me. It's happening. The door's ... Yes. He's in. And ... I ... er ... I don't think it's Sergio Treize. No. It's an older man. Never seen him before. He's got a holdall in his hand. He's near you. He's put it down and ... He's got out one of those cooled boxes for storing body organs. He's our man. He's put that down as well. He's got something else in his right hand. A knife. Scalpel. Keep still, Lexi. He's put the scalpel on top of the box. He's got a jemmy – you know, a crowbar – out of the bag and he's examining the coffin lid. He's going to lever it. Hold your breath. He's realized it's not sealed. He's putting the crowbar down. He's pushing the lid back now. No weapon in his hand.'

Troy's chest felt tight, about to burst. He didn't know what Lexi was going through. He didn't know how she could be so static and so serene that she could be mistaken for a corpse. At least in dim lighting.

Hardly daring to communicate at all, he whispered faintly, 'He's … Well, you can feel it, can't you?' The man was undoing her robe. 'You're okay. He hasn't picked up the … He is now, I think. Get ready. Yes, he's reaching for the scalpel. That's enough, Lexi. Finish it.'

But she didn't. She just lay there.

Troy swallowed and stared at the screen. Had his partner slipped into unconsciousness? Was she aware of what was about to happen? Could she defend herself?

Lexi waited. Waited till the fine metal blade touched her flesh. Then she made her move. Her eyes opened and she thrust her right arm upwards. Her fist slammed against his throat and the scalpel flew across the room.

The man leapt back in panic. His crazed scream filled the hall with shrill sound, like a seagull's cry. Terrified, his eyes were wide and white. Clutching his injured neck, he squealed, 'Don't hurt me!'

Gathering the robe around her body, Lexi dragged herself up, elbows on the sides of the coffin. She snorted. 'Me hurt *you*? You were about to cut my heart out!'

Troy appeared in the entrance. But the intruder wasn't going to make a bid for freedom. Shock had immobilized him entirely. Into his life-logger, Troy said, 'I need an immediate police escort at Hurlstone's hall of rest. One man to be arrested, questioned and charged.'

SCENE 26

Saturday 12th April, Late night

The man that Troy and Lexi had arrested sat across the table from them in the interview room. He was about sixty, they guessed, and his hand occasionally drifted to his throat to soothe the pain of Lexi's punch. On the floor lay his holdall, but anything that could have been used as a weapon had already been removed. The contents of his pockets were scattered across the surface of the table.

'For the sake of the recording,' Troy said, 'tell us your name.'

'Ely Dean Eight.'

For a few moments, Troy looked puzzled. Then he said, 'Of course. Dr Ely Eight. You used to be the house surgeon at the Rural Retreat Transplant Clinic.'

'Yes. Retired.'

'Gianna Humble mentioned you.' Seeing a reaction in the doctor's face, Troy said, 'You don't like her.'

'She said I was too old. She accused me of being a bit forgetful and shaky.'

Troy smiled. 'Ah. I get it.' He lifted the cooled container out of the surgeon's holdall and said, 'You couldn't retire gracefully, could you? You're not in the black market for money. You're trying to prove her wrong. You're trying to prove you've still got it.'

'I'm perfectly able to help desperately ill people.'

'Are you? Wasn't Gianna right? You've made mistakes – like Olga Wylie.'

Refusing to reply, Ely stared at the table.

'Do you remember her? She got an outer's heart. It belonged to Tiffany Clara One and it was stolen from the same hall of rest.'

'There were two patients,' Ely mumbled. 'There was a mix-up. I was given the wrong ones.'

'So, there's another body somewhere. We only found Olga.' Troy leaned forward on the table. 'Who gave you the wrong heart?'

'Um. Nobody.'

Troy sat back again. 'You're facing a lot of charges. Unlawful killing, mutilation of bodies, prevention of proper burial or cremation, and it might include murder.'

Ely jerked upright and stared at Troy. 'I haven't murdered anyone.'

'So, who has? Who's your accomplice?'

Ely shook his head.

'What's the deal? You do the skilled work – the surgery on the living and the dead – and someone else does the rough stuff, like murdering the vulnerable and getting rid of embarrassing bodies – or what remains of them.'

Still no reply.

'How did you hear about Lexi's death?'

Ely Eight kept his silence again.

Troy took Ely's mobile in his hand. 'I'm betting that earlier tonight – maybe just after seven thirty – you had a call from your accomplice suggesting you pay another visit to the hall of rest.' He fiddled with the phone and then smiled. 'Here we go. A call came in at seven forty-seven and it was someone listed as Samaritan according to this.' Troy glanced at Lexi and passed the phone to her.

At once, she called Terabyte. 'We need the owner

and location of a mobile. And we need it fast. Here's the number.' She dictated Samaritan's phone number and then said, 'Thanks. I'll be waiting.'

Troy gazed at Ely in silence for ten uncomfortable seconds. 'It won't be long. Our friend's a genius with phones.' He tapped the side of his head and said, 'I'm building up a picture in here. I can see how your relationship with Samaritan works. He's not like you. Big pockets. They take a lot of filling. That's why he deals in black-market body parts. Money's his motivation. Expensive lifestyle to support, I should think. So he covers up your mistakes to protect his business. He might even be threatening to expose you if you tell someone like me who he is – or if you really retire. He's basically a greedy bully, isn't he?'

Ely's eyes were filling up with tears.

'You can tell us who he is because it won't make any difference to you any more. You're safe in here and your phone's going to lead us to him anyway.'

Barely audible, Ely said, 'His name's Gareth Riley Thirteen.'

At once, Lexi checked the case files on her life-logger. 'Gareth Riley Thirteen holds a fishing licence for the Shepford area.'

Troy nodded and looked once more at Ely Eight. 'How did you meet him?'

'He did the techie jobs at the Rural Retreat when I was there. He set up the computer system.'

'The failsafe procedure with barcodes? The one that makes accidents impossible?'

'Yes.'

'Pity he didn't set you up with the same system in your ... private clinic.'

'We don't have the resources.'

'Where is it? Where do you do the transplants?'

'In my basement at home. It's fully equipped.'

Lexi made a note of Ely's address, out in the countryside beyond Langhorn and Overdale.

'Is Gareth still at the Rural Retreat?'

'He was sacked for misusing computers.'

'Meaning?'

Between sobs, Ely replied, 'He was caught a few too many times in chat rooms and the like when he should've been working.'

Lexi interrupted. 'We've got a location. He's at home.'

'Okay. Let's go and prick his balloon.' Troy stood up and told Ely, 'We'll talk some more later. For now, it's a police cell.'

Lexi added, 'More comfortable than a coffin, believe me.'

SCENE 27

Saturday 12th April, Midnight

'Lexi Iona Four,' Troy said. 'You're … '

'What? A star?'

'A good partner.'

'Is that all? Only good?'

Troy's cheeks reddened. 'Well, I was going to say brave and brilliant but, given what you just did, I think I'll stick with dead good.'

Lexi smiled. 'If we're into compliments, you're doing all right – for a major. Better than my last partner.'

'Thanks.'

Outside, the few lamps of Langhorn hardly made an impression on the darkness. As they swept past the reservoir on the main road, Troy picked out the glow from the Rural Retreat Transplant Clinic and a distant glimmer that might have marked the lakeside position of Avril Smallcross's house or the nearby water treatment office. Silhouettes of trees chopped the lights, making them appear to wink on and off as the car headed for the community of Overdale beyond.

'Do you reckon we're on our way to a chat with Sergio Treize?' Lexi asked, tapping the keys of her life-logger at the same time.

'Probably.'

'How many different names can one man have?'

'Just remember,' Troy said, 'whatever he's called, he's perfectly capable of clobbering someone over the head with a blunt object and slitting the odd throat or two.'

'Terabyte says he's lost the phone signal. We don't know where he is any more.'

'Perhaps he was expecting to hear from Ely by now. Maybe he knows something's gone wrong so he's smashed his phone to make sure no one can trace it.'

When Overdale first came into view, it was a dome

of diffuse yellow light. As they got closer, they began to distinguish curved lines of lamplight that defined the streets of the community.

Lexi lifted up her life-logger and showed Troy a photograph. It was the fountain outside the Rural Retreat Transplant Clinic and two rows of people were posing in front of it. 'I found this. The caption says it was taken to mark the clinic's opening ceremony,' she told him. 'No information but, look, there's Ely Eight – in his innocent period, when he could still hold a scalpel steady. And Gianna. Check out the back, though. Imagine this man without hair but with white glasses. That's a good likeness of Sergio Treize.'

Troy shrugged. 'Is it?'

'There's not enough definition for a conclusive result from facial recognition software, but it doesn't rule him out.'

'If you chop his hair off but don't add glasses, it could be a younger Kofi Seven.'

Lexi studied the image again. 'Well, now you mention it … But forget it. Kofi's on our side.'

Gareth Riley Thirteen did not live in one of the regular properties. The car took Troy and Lexi to the west of Overdale's main residential zone and up to the entrance of a separate stone building. The iron gate didn't open automatically so they got out and surveyed the house and its garden. The drive swerved in front of the house and led to a large garage to one side. Attached to the front of Gareth's home, three spotlights blazed, but the curtains and windows were not brightened by internal lamps.

'Asleep or not in,' Lexi guessed.

'If he knows we're on his tail … '

'He'll have gone – or he's lying in wait for us.'

'Not good either way.' Troy shuddered in the cold night air.

'Let's get on with it,' Lexi prompted, walking away from the gate. 'The wall's easy to climb this way.'

She was right. It was a jagged dry-stone wall providing plenty of grips and toeholds. In a few seconds, they had both clambered up and jumped down onto a large neat lawn. Striding towards the front door, Troy felt exposed. 'If he's at one of the windows with a gun … '

'Duck.'

'Yeah. If he's only got one bullet, that'll do the trick.'

'It's dark,' Lexi replied. 'He'll miss. Anyway, life-loggers are a good defence. Not many bad guys attack when they know everything's being monitored.'

They didn't remain in the shadows. They soon found themselves within the glow of the spotlight over the door. But no one fired at them. There was no sound except the quiet groaning of an oak tree as it swayed in the wind.

There was no response to Troy's ringing of the doorbell. There was no response to a hefty bang on the door either.

The two detectives looked at each other and Lexi said, 'We can only break in if we think someone's in danger or if we're sure we can prevent a serious crime.'

Aware that their life-loggers would be used to make sure that they had acted correctly, Troy answered formally, 'I'm sure there'll be evidence that'll help us stop more mutilations and maybe murders.'

'Me too.'

Lexi examined the door and took a step backwards, ready to kick her way in. Her right leg flew forward at amazing speed and crashed against the panel nearest the lock. Wood splintered and the door sprang back. 'Well, if he's in, he knows we're on our way.' Before entering, she said, 'You watch my back and I'll watch yours. Okay?'

'Okay.'

She hesitated in the hallway, next to the light switch. 'I don't know about you, but I prefer to see where I'm going – and what clues are on offer.'

'And who's lurking in the corner with a great big knife.'

Lexi turned on the lamps to reveal a large but cluttered entrance. At once, she made for a small wooden shoe rack. Bending down and speaking in a hush, she said, 'Size twelves, but those Adiboks aren't here.' She stood up again and glanced around. 'No one with a knife.'

'So far.'

'Let's see if we can sort out his identity.' Treading softly, she made for the door at the end of the passage.

'It'd be a good idea to check the bedrooms first – in case he's asleep upstairs,' Troy whispered.

With a sly grin, Lexi nodded. 'I tend to rummage for clues first, forgetting the obvious way of finding things out – like taking a look at his face.' She crept up the staircase with Troy.

They didn't need to speak. They checked out each room in silence, communicating with glances and gestures. Troy pushed each door aside gently and Lexi peered inside. Of the three bedrooms, two had unmade beds. They were clearly unused. The other was Gareth's but the bed was empty. The bathroom was also vacant.

'He's downstairs,' Lexi muttered, 'or not here at all.'

The living room was ordinary. A sofa and two easy chairs, a shelf of trinkets above the gas fire, a coffee table, a music centre, a large rubber plant to the side of a bay window. In daylight, Gareth would have good views over the countryside. Troy peered behind the sofa and all other possible hiding places, but found no one ready to pounce on them. Lexi was drawn to the piles of possessions and let out a contented murmur. From among the trinkets, she extracted a ring. Threading it on her pen so she could examine it without touching, she said, 'Hey presto. One blue stone missing.' She let the ring slide off the pen and into a small evidence bag.

'Nice,' Troy whispered.

'I'll get a team in here tomorrow. There might be more.'

'What's the betting there's Icelandic death metal downloaded onto the music system?'

Lexi nodded. 'I'll get that checked as well.'

They tiptoed back along the hallway, checking the downstairs toilet and kitchen as they went. 'The sink's not wet,' Troy said, 'and there's no food or drink left out.'

When they went into the final room, Lexi turned on the light and gasped.

Troy groaned.

It was a well-equipped computer room but it looked as if it had been thoroughly trashed. Broken circuit boards and damaged hard drives were scattered over the messy bench. There was also a mobile phone, mangled and minus its battery.

'Looks to me like an attempt to wipe electronic evidence,' said Troy.

'Yeah, but why?'

Now that they had been in every room, convinced that Gareth was not inside the house, Troy spoke up. 'First, a detective keeps calling him about his chat room and then – maybe – Ely doesn't make an agreed contact after his raid on the hall of rest.'

Lexi gazed at the fragments of electronic components. 'I wonder if any of these came from Olga's or Dmitri's computer. I'll get Terabyte to examine everything in the morning. If this was a hurried job – not as thorough as it might have been – there'll still be some usable bits. By the time Terabyte's finished, we'll know more about Gareth Riley Thirteen.' She looked at the monitor and then followed the line of sight of its tiny camera. She pointed to the wall opposite. 'Could be where he took your video calls. I'll check out the background – behind his head – in the recordings. There might be a colour match or a mark that confirms it. Best done in daylight tomorrow. For now … '

'Yes. More than anything, we need to find him.'

Lexi thought for a moment. 'You know, a poorly outer could be waiting for my heart. He could be with a patient.'

'That'd be Ely's house. But if he knows we're on to him … '

Lexi shrugged. 'The basement clinic's likely to be our main crime scene, so I want to go there anyway.'

'Okay.'

Before they left, they broke into the side door of the double garage. Once the long strip light had flickered into life, they saw that one half of the space was empty. The rest was occupied by a vintage car under restoration. Troy smiled and said, 'That's the reason Sharon Angie bought car parts.'

'Yeah. Sharon equals Sergio equals Gareth Thirteen.' Lexi paused before adding, 'Big expensive house and vintage car. Now we know why he needed money from the transplant trade.'

They arranged for uniformed officers to guard the house and then returned to their own car.

SCENE 28

Sunday 13th April, The early hours

Even before they got close to Ely Eight's isolated house, its location was obvious. It was ablaze. Giant flames were clawing at the night sky, replacing the darkness with constantly shifting yellowy-orange streaks. The fire was so fierce that, even before Lexi got out of the car, she suspected arson. It looked as if it had been started with a lot of fuel to cause maximum damage. It was consuming the house hungrily.

Troy and Lexi ran towards the inferno but they were soon brought to a halt by intense heat. Above the roar, Lexi shouted, 'Look. It's worst in the basement. That's probably where it began. I can't smell any fuel, can you?'

'No.'

'If someone splashed it around, it might have all burnt by now. I don't know how long it's been going. Quite a while, because the whole house is going up. Amazing.'

'My guess is it's an attempt to destroy all evidence of an underground clinic – or at least Gareth's part in it.'

A downstairs window exploded and flame leapt out angrily. A large part of the roof fell in, sending tiles crashing down.

'My main crime scene burnt to a crisp,' Lexi moaned.

Hearing a distant siren, Troy said, 'Firefighters on their way.'

She shrugged. 'What's going to be left?'

Four appliances pulled up outside Ely's house. The chief dashed towards the detectives and yelled, 'Is anyone inside?'

'The owner's away but we don't know about anyone else,' Troy answered. 'I hope not.'

'There could be gas cylinders in the basement because it was used as a surgery,' Lexi told him.

‘Okay. Thanks. Now keep back,’ he ordered. ‘This is our job.’

SCENE 29

Sunday 13th April, Pre-dawn

Troy lay back in the tilted car seat. His body was tired but his brain would not allow sleep. It galloped along, thinking endlessly about the case and this latest turn of events. Lexi had let go of her mind. It was drifting wherever it wanted to go, like a feather floating on a breeze in a place where nothing happened. She was at rest. When the chief fire officer roused them, Troy was still focused but weary. Lexi was raring to go.

The firefighters had erected a cordon around what remained of Ely's property. Much of it had been reduced to charcoal. The blackened joists that had once supported the roof were exposed like the bones of a skeleton.

'What caused it?' Troy asked the chief.

'Too early to say, but it wasn't an accident. It was just too severe. My guess is forensics will find an accelerant.'

'I need to get into the basement,' Lexi said.

'No. It's too dangerous.'

'But ... '

'I'm overruling you,' the chief firefighter said. 'I don't want any more casualties.'

'Any more?' Troy queried.

He nodded. 'There's a body in the basement. Well, I say body but there's not a lot left.'

Troy and Lexi glanced at each other.

'Your officers have been inside, then. So, I'm going in, as well,' Lexi insisted.

'They've got the right clothing and a lot of training.'

Lexi held out her arms. 'Bet you've got a spare set of gear that'll fit me.'

'But I haven't got a couple of years to train you.'

'Come in with me,' she replied. Putting a hand on her life-logger, she added, 'I need to record this body and I'm hoping there's still a bit of equipment I can measure.'

'Nothing's safe in there. Not even the walls.'

'That makes it doubly important I get in now. It might have collapsed before we can get forensic fire specialists in.'

'Well ... '

'This is a multiple murder investigation. We might have the culprit in there – a casualty of his own crime – or another victim.'

'All right. Against my better judgement.'

While the chief helped Lexi into protective clothing, she said to Troy, 'I reckon it's Sergio Treize. He knew we were onto him and he chose not to get caught and prosecuted. He stayed in there deliberately, taking a way out that's familiar to someone in charge of a suicide chat room.'

'Mmm.' Troy tapped at the keypad of his life-logger. 'Maybe.'

'I'm giving us three minutes at most,' the chief said to her. 'We go in, you video what you want, and we're back out. Understand? You do exactly what I say. No arguments. No lingering.'

'Okay.'

Troy watched his partner, weighed down by firefighting gear and breathing apparatus, trudging awkwardly beside the chief. Both of them scouted out a route by torchlight. Troy couldn't fault her dedication and bravery. He hoped that her recklessness would not get her into trouble. He prayed that the walls would remain upright for another three minutes.

Lexi and the chief firefighter emerged from the wreck after three and a half minutes.

While Lexi cast aside the safety gear, like an insect struggling to shed its cocoon, she said, 'I've got what I want. The body's got big feet, too burnt to get an accurate measure or to decide if it's an outer. I got some tissue to test, though. But the big news is a gurney. That's the other thing I went in for. Its metal frame's a bit warped but I still got an accurate fix on the wheelbase. Fifty-two centimetres. Exactly the same as the tracks in the field by the bodies.'

Troy nodded. 'Good work. And you're still alive as well.'

She smiled. 'That's an added bonus.' Handing the breathing apparatus to one of the crew, she said, 'Actually, I like dressing up. And excitement. I've always fancied being a firefighter.' She inhaled the air, polluted by the powerful whiff of combustion products. 'We'll see, but I think this case is all over. I reckon Sergio took the easy way out.'

Hesitating, Troy muttered, 'That'd be convenient. But ... '

'What?'

The first light of Sunday had not y
the horizon. As they made their way caref
the car, Troy said, 'The airport's about fifty ki
away. And there's an early morning fligh
Switzerland. I've stopped it. The passengers think the pilot's ill and they're waiting for a replacement.'

'Why … ?'

'Because Sergio Treize – or Gareth Thirteen or whatever you want to call him – doesn't seem to me to be the quitting kind. And he's always a step ahead of us.' He stopped and showed her a picture. 'It's a still from a camera at Gate Thirty-Two, the one the Swiss flight's leaving from.'

'And?'

'Look at the man by the pillar. He's got hair – a wig, maybe – a day's growth of stubble and no glasses, but … '

Lexi peered at the photo. 'That's a lot of ifs and buts. And nowhere near the resolution you'd need for a facial recognition program. Have you checked the passenger list?'

'No familiar names, but he seems to have plenty up his sleeve. I don't know what's on his passport.'

'If you're right, who's that in Ely Eight's house?'

'No idea,' Troy admitted. 'But it could be the

patient who was going to get your heart. I imagine your forensics will tell us … '

'It'll be a challenge after what the tissue and bones have been through.'

'You'll sort it out.' Less confidently, Troy added, 'Maybe Sergio left the body as a decoy, so we'd … '

Lexi interrupted, 'Think exactly what I thought?'

Troy nodded. 'The wrong tree, for barking up.'

'You weren't wasting time while I was having fun in a hot, toxic and unstable ruin.' She examined the image from the airport again. 'I'm not convinced, though.'

'Neither am I,' Troy said. 'But you have to admit … '

'I have to admit you won't give up and go to your bed until you're sure one way or the other.'

'Less than a week and you're getting to know me.'

In the car, Lexi said firmly, 'The airport.'

SCENE 30

Sunday 13th April, Early morning

At the airport, Troy told the Head of Security about the passenger he wanted to interview. He asked for a ring of security guards around the wing that housed Gate 32. 'Every conceivable exit, please. The public ones and the staff-only ones. Access to shafts or whatever. If he does a runner, he mustn't get away.'

'That's not one of the scenarios we've practised, but it's straightforward enough. I'll have that section sealed within five minutes.'

'We'll hang on,' Troy decided. 'Tell me when a mouse couldn't escape, then we'll move in.'

Troy and Lexi went through the departure lounge to Gate 30 and waited for the signal that all the guards were in place. From where they stood, Troy could just hear a calming announcement in the neighbouring area. A sympathetic voice was apologising for the disruption to the flight, reassuring a restless bunch of travellers that a pilot was nearly ready and that they would be able to board the aircraft very soon. It was clear to Troy that the crew was as much in the dark as the passengers. The man making the announcement had probably not been told there was a different reason for delaying the departure. If Sergio Treize was among the impatient travellers, Troy didn't know whether he would be anxious, suspicious or enraged. Whatever his emotion, he'd be dangerous.

The message transmitted to Troy's life-logger was simple. *All officers in place.* Troy took a deep breath and nodded at Lexi. Side-by-side and without a word, they strode a few paces down the terminal corridor and entered Gate 32.

Immediately, a passenger at the far side of the area jumped to his feet. It was the man Troy suspected of being Sergio Treize. Eyes wild, he glanced around, assessing the situation. He would have seen two detectives blocking the entrance and two beefy guards blocking the way to the aircraft. He would have realized at once that he was trapped.

Quick-witted, though, he worked out a way of escaping that Troy hadn't anticipated. He plucked a girl – about five years old – from the seat in front of him. He held her up effortlessly with his left arm and shouted, 'Stand back. You're going to let me walk – or she gets it.' A sudden spasm made his head jerk.

The girl lashed out, trying to scratch his face. She succeeded only in removing his wig. She was so astonished by the disappearance of her captor's hair that she didn't continue the struggle. She screamed and then sobbed in the direction of her distraught mother or nanny.

Troy saw a facial resemblance between the girl and the woman so he guessed that they were daughter and mother. He stepped forward to face Sergio Treize. 'I don't think you want to do this. You're on enough charges already. No judge is lenient with anybody who threatens a child. And you can't escape.'

'Wrong. You've got nothing on me and if you want this kid back in one piece … '

The passengers had forgotten about their flight. They were absorbed by the drama taking place among them, horrified, silent. Apart from the girl's mother. She began to wail and suddenly darted at

Sergio. She didn't stand a chance. Still encircling the girl with his left arm, he punched the mother with his right. It was vicious and precise, almost professional. She staggered back and fell onto a seat, completely dazed. The other travellers gasped.

Troy looked directly into Sergio's face. He saw a man who was determined and utterly ruthless. He wasn't bluffing. Maybe he twitched because he was always tense – on the verge of an explosive temper.

Talking to the girl, Troy asked, 'What's your name?'

Through the tears and the choking, she spluttered, 'Melanie.'

'All right, Melanie. I need you to stay calm. Your mum's fine. Just a bit wobbly. I'll make sure you're back with her soon. Okay? I promise. Just do as the man says. Don't do anything to make him angry.'

Sergio smirked at Troy. 'Nice speech. Wise words. Now, contact security and use some more wise words. Clear the way for me. Go on. Take your own advice. Do what the man says. Don't make him angry.'

Troy wished he knew more about his partner. He wished he'd learned to read Lexi's mind. Would she be doing some crazy calculation, balancing the value of catching a killer against the life of a child? Or would she have some brilliant idea? Troy knew only his own mind. Catching a killer wasn't worth the risk to any child. 'All right,' he said hesitantly.

Sergio grinned widely. 'There's no problem with our pilot, is there? That was make-believe. So I want this flight in the air in fifteen minutes. Understand? The girl stays with me. I'll release her when I've touched down, beyond your reach.'

'Better go along with it,' Lexi said. 'I'll go and sort it out with the manager.'

So, Lexi did have a plan. Troy didn't know what it was but he was sure she had no intention of allowing Sergio Treize to flee from the law and win his freedom in Switzerland.

Within minutes, the crew announced the boarding of the flight. Before Sergio and Melanie joined the queue, Troy checked his life-logger and nodded at them. 'You've got the all-clear to go. No one'll stop you.'

Sergio laughed as he joined the other passengers. 'You're not sure your partner's doing the right thing, are you? Letting me go. But she is – if you want the kid back safe and sound.'

Troy did not reply. If the stakes had not been so high, he would have found the comment amusing. Sergio had got the two of them entirely wrong. It was

Troy who would trade a killer's freedom for a girl's life. It was Lexi who'd be tempted to do something rash. Troy assumed that was exactly what she was planning as the murderer walked down the loading bridge and onto the aircraft.

He bound towards the crew's desk and said, 'Are there cameras on board? Can I see what's happening?'

'Sure.'

A steward set up the monitor and Troy watched the usual chaos as passengers found their seats and pushed hand luggage into overhead lockers. One of the cabin crew was helping Melanie's mother into her seat on the left-hand side of the aeroplane. In a few minutes, though, everyone was in place and ready for take-off.

There was no sign of Lexi in the lounge or on the aircraft.

The plane broke free of its passenger-loading bridge and slowly reversed away from the terminal. Then it spun round to face the other way and began the long taxi to the runway.

'What's happening?' Troy muttered to himself, wiping the sweat from his brow. 'I'm sure she ... '

He watched on screen as two stewards walked down each aisle to check that all the travellers had buckled their safety belts properly across their laps. Near the camera that Troy was monitoring, Sergio Treize and his hostage were sitting next to each other on the right-hand side of the fuselage, well away from Melanie's mother. Melanie was on the inside and Sergio occupied the aisle seat. The remnants of a smile were still on his face.

But then Troy saw the crew member who was coming up behind him to inspect his seat belt. Troy gulped as he recognized Lexi in the airline's uniform. Immediately, he realized what she had planned. She'd decided to tackle him once he'd put his hostage to one side and fastened himself into a seat. She must have calculated that she'd have enough of an advantage because he'd be locked into a cramped space and taken by surprise.

At that moment, though, Troy remembered Terabyte reporting that Sharon Angie had bought books on martial arts. He wished he could warn Lexi that Sergio Treize could be an expert fighter. Yet there was no time and no way of whispering in her ear. He could only gaze at a screen and pray.

Lexi stepped forward and her clenched fist came out of the blue.

SCENE 31

Sunday 13th April, Morning

Even as the plane taxied away from the terminal, Sergio Treize was alert. His seat belt wasn't buckled. He had laid it across his lap so it looked fastened, but he was prepared for any attempt to arrest him. When he saw Lexi's fist, he lurched instinctively to the side. His lightning-fast reaction saved him from the full force of her punch. Athletically, he sprang into the aisle and faced her.

Lexi knew already that he was a formidable opponent. She had recognized the immobilizing punch that he'd used on Melanie's mother.

Inhaling, she adopted her favourite sidewise high stance.

With superior height and reach, Sergio unleashed a brutal strike aimed at her jaw.

Lexi put up a knife-hand block and used her momentum to chop at the side of his neck. She knew the hit would have been painful but it wouldn't disable him.

He twisted and directed a kick at her upper right leg. She slid her foot across the limited floor space to dodge the blow and, with practised timing, slipped her right hand under his heel and thrust it upwards. She hoped to make him fall flat on his back, but Sergio was cunning and slippery. He lurched backwards but nimbly kept on his feet.

Steadying himself, he smiled and said, 'You're good.' Immediately, he launched a straight punch to her solar plexus.

Lexi stepped to the left and her thigh crashed into the side of a seat. Impeded, she couldn't deflect the blow with the outside of her right arm. For a moment, she thought that the strike hadn't injured her. But she soon realized that she was struggling to breathe. She did her best not to show her discomfort, though. She didn't want to encourage him.

She parried his next blow but a knife-hand strike

came crashing into her upper right arm. Straightaway, she felt the damage to her muscle.

With a twitch of his head, Sergio sneered. 'But not good enough.'

He allowed her to land a punch on his body to show that she had lost much of the power in her right arm.

Lexi glanced beyond him and knew what she had to do. She could take him if only she could drive him backwards again. She relaxed her posture, feigning an attitude of defeat, because this time she did want to encourage him. He came at her with a low kick. She parried it and, surprising him, moved inside his defences, pummelling him with short stabs. They were never going to overwhelm him. They didn't have to. Her attack simply needed to be uncomfortable and annoying.

It worked because he shuffled his legs, moving away from her flurry of blows.

And that's when he fell over Melanie who had curled up into a tight ball on the floor of the aisle.

His head cracked against the foot of one of the seats. Lexi jumped over Melanie and, to make sure, delivered a knock-out punch to his right temple. It shut down his brain in an instant.

Straightaway, Lexi turned to Melanie and asked, 'Are you all right?'

The girl nodded.

'Thanks, Melanie. Nice move. I remember it from school. Always good to use on a bully.'

'Nasty man.'

Lexi took Melanie's hand and, as the passengers clapped and cheered, took her to her still groggy mother. 'There was a mix-up in seat numbers,' Lexi said with a grin. 'I think Melanie should be next to you.' Then she shouted to everyone, 'Sorry, folks. We're going back to the terminal. You've got one too many passengers on board.'

SCENE 32

Sunday 13th April, Mid-morning

Security staff had boarded the aeroplane and taken Sergio Treize to the airport holding cell. At Lexi's request, his clothing and a sample of DNA were taken while he was out cold. It was an hour before he regained consciousness and another hour before a doctor gave Troy and Lexi the go-ahead to interview him.

Troy was ragged and exhausted but eager to talk to the man with so many different names. 'You don't look like a Sharon,' he began.

Wearing a prison uniform, Sergio ignored the

comment. Instead, he stared at Lexi. Almost snarling, he said, 'You'll be hurting.'

'Yes, but I can walk out of here after we've had a chat. You're not going anywhere.'

'What tripped me up?'

'Never underestimate little girls. Resourceful creatures. And vindictive if you get on their wrong side.' Lexi looked down at his shoes and said, 'Nice trainers. I checked out the tread while you were sleeping it off.'

Troy took over. 'The same prints turned up at three graves next to Langhorn Reservoir.'

Sergio laughed. 'Well done. You've just proved that I go fishing there sometimes.'

'And they were at Olga Wylie's place.'

'Who's Olga Wylie?'

Troy smiled. 'She's the person you and Ely Eight killed with a heart mix-up. Ely's admitted it – and told us about you. Olga's also the woman you burgled. You left a sapphire from your ring in her study.'

'A stone that could have been from my ring turns up at a burgled house? It could have come from any bit of jewellery in the same range. How does that prove I've committed murder? You don't have any real evidence. Nothing.' Sergio hesitated and added,

'Just the ramblings of a crazy old surgeon who lost his last job because he was unreliable and forgetful. Not an ideal witness.'

'If you hadn't burnt down Ely's house, we'd have sown it up by now,' Troy replied with an unconcerned shrug. 'So, we're going to have to give it a bit more welly.'

'What are you talking about?'

'My partner's got a way with words,' Lexi explained. 'I think he means we've got to try harder.'

'No problem,' Troy said to Sergio. 'I'll get you moved to a police cell and in twenty-four hours we'll speak again. That's all we'll need to knock you off your perch.'

For a fraction of a second, a worried expression flashed across Sergio's face. His nervous tic made his head jolt to the side.

'You see,' Troy continued, 'there's another crime scene you forgot to destroy. The van you no doubt used like an ambulance. You abandoned it here at the airport. I've had officers all over the car park and they've found it. It looks beautifully clean. I bet you thought cleaning was enough.' He turned to his bruised partner and asked, 'What do you think?'

'I think cleaning's never enough. There's always a trace and I'll find the smallest scraps.'

Troy stood up. 'For now, you're charged with assault and child abduction – in front of almost two hundred witnesses. Tomorrow, it'll be multiple murder.'

SCENE 33

Monday 14th April, Morning

Troy had cleansed himself in the temple and asked for the strength to handle the final interview. He had also refreshed himself with sleep, meatballs and chocolate. While Lexi and a squad of forensic scientists had taken care of all the clever stuff, Troy had given the order to release Huw from Foreditch Crime Central and prepared himself mentally. Then, immediately before his verbal battle with Sergio Treize, he'd been briefed by Lexi. He'd heard all about her team's successes – and its failures.

In one of the cells in Shepford Crime Central,

Sergio's hands and ankles were clasped together with plastic ties because, during his move from the airport to Shepford, he'd attacked a policewoman in an attempt to escape. It had taken three more officers to restrain him.

Troy nodded towards the bindings and said, 'For someone claiming to be innocent, you seem very keen to make a break for it.' With barely a pause, he asked, 'What do you know about Franki Savannah Fifteen?'

'Nothing,' Sergio replied.

'Mmm. We don't know much either. Yet.'

Lexi said, 'You did a pretty good job on the clinic and whoever was inside. It's going to take a bit longer for me to extract DNA from the bone and the pathologist to work out the cause of death.'

'But,' Troy put in, 'a bit of research tells us Franki Savannah Fifteen is a promising tennis player with a heart complaint. She's also an outer, wealthy and missing.'

Sergio shrugged. 'No idea.'

'Why were there traces of fuel on your clothing yesterday?'

'I've got a vintage car. I was putting petrol in it. I sloshed some over the side and had to clear it up.'

'Yes. Of course you did.' Troy twisted and turned, probing the man sitting opposite him at the table.

'You're Gareth Riley Thirteen, but you're Sergio Treize and a whole lot of other people as well. Customs tells us your passport's forged. It's lucky I can charge you under any name.'

'And your point is?'

'You didn't destroy every bit of your computer memory. Your internet history shows you're Sergio Treize who looks after a suicide chat room and posts messages as Charon Angel.'

'I still don't get it.'

'There was a mark on the wall behind where you sit. Just for a split-second – when you moved – the same mark appears in the video the first time I called you.'

'What does that prove?' Sergio shook his head. 'I'm not impressed by you two.'

'At least we haven't been outwitted by a five-year-old on a plane. Anyway, I'm taking it a step at a time. You're not denying that you're these different people, that the computer's yours.'

Sergio shrugged.

'How do you explain the fact that Dmitri Backhouse's and Olga Wylie's hard drives are in your house?'

He twitched before answering, 'They're not.'

Troy smiled. 'Along with a lot of other electronic

junk, they're in the bin. After you drilled holes through them, they're unreadable. I'll give you that. But our computer guy got serial numbers off them. One was bought by Dmitri and the other belonged to Olga.'

'I've got no idea how they ended up at my place.'

This time, Troy saw a weakness, a crack in his defences. The merest flicker of his eyes told Troy that he was nervous. 'There's a spade at your house. It's got a bit of soil on it. Lexi's done all the microscopic stuff. The quartz grains match the earth at Langhorn. That suggests to me you've been digging holes there.'

With only a moment's hesitation, Sergio replied, 'Too right. I dig up earthworms as bait.'

Troy nodded. 'Exactly what I'd say. What do you catch?'

'Not a lot. Roach and the occasional perch.'

'Do you eat them?'

'No. It's for sport.'

'Of course, you're an outer. You're more likely to scoff the maggots.'

'I just told you. I use worms.'

'Oh, that's right. Sorry. I forgot you said that.'

Sergio sighed. He was both weary and wary of Troy.

'Let's move on to the last crime scene. There's a

mat in the back of your van, ambulance or whatever you want to call it. Why is there a trace of fuel soaked into it?'

'That'll be spillage. You know, when I got that can of petrol for my restoration job.'

'Not the fuel you took to the clinic – to help you burn it down, along with Franki Savannah Fifteen?'

His head convulsed. 'No.'

Troy knew by instinct that the time was right to go for the killer punch. 'Tell me, how come we found DNA from Olga Wylie, Jerome Sebastian Eleven and Dmitri Backhouse under the mat in the van?'

'It's not my van. It belongs to Ely Eight. Ask him.'

'That's strange, because you just said you used the van. To get a can of petrol.'

'So, I borrowed it this once.'

'Mmm. Well, we don't have your fingerprints all over it – or on anything else – for the obvious reason. You're an outer.' Troy turned towards Lexi and said, 'But whose DNA did you find all around the driver's seat?'

'His,' she said, nodding towards Sergio Treize.

'Anyone else's? Like Ely Eight's?'

'No.'

'That's weird, isn't it?' Troy said, looking again at Sergio. 'How do you explain that?'

'Er … '

'You're trying to blame Ely Eight but you were the only driver.'

Sergio's hands were in his lap, under the table. In a sudden swell of anger, he smashed them upwards, expecting to thrust the table at Troy. He didn't realize that it was screwed securely into the floor and would not budge. He cried out in pain and frustration. Instead, he lifted his tied hands up high and crashed them down on the table top. The wood split under the force of his blow.

Realizing that he was right about Sergio's explosive temper, Troy rose to his feet. 'You're charged with the murders of Dmitri Backhouse and Jerome Sebastian Eleven, and the unlawful killing of Olga Wylie. There'll be others as well.' He pointed to the table and said, 'Like damage to police property.' Wiping away his smile, he added, 'And when we work out what happened to Franki Savannah Fifteen. I'm legally obliged to read you a complete list when we've got it all figured out.'

Lexi stood next to her partner and said, 'The blue stone we found in Olga Wylie's house – close to where she kept her computer – matches the others in your ring. That's a charge of burglary as well. And I've got more bad news for you.' With a wicked grin on her face, she told him, 'Those sapphires aren't sapphires. They're cheap fakes. You were ripped off.'

SCENE 34

Monday 14th April, Noon

Below them, the gentle splashing sound came from the fountain outside the Rural Retreat Transplant Clinic. Lexi had retrieved her spy cameras and she was sitting on the earth next to Troy, lapping up the peaceful atmosphere. They were enjoying the feeling of being in the wood but not having dead bodies – or parts of dead bodies – to dig up and investigate.

Breathing in the fresh air, Troy said, 'I can see the attraction for the patients, Avril Smallcross and Huw.'

'Yeah. Nature – and doing nothing – is great for

fifteen minutes. Then you'd get bored and want some life.'

'I suppose. Anyway, I've got batteries to recharge. I'm going home for a bit. Back to Grandma's.'

Lexi glanced at her partner. 'You live with your grandmother, not your parents?'

Troy brought the shutter down on the topic abruptly. 'Yes.'

'Okay. I'll go and hang out with friends. I'd ask you along but ... '

Troy smiled. 'I wouldn't mix.'

'Some of them think majors have only just crawled out of the swamps.'

'That's all right. I'll keep a good distance between you and Grandma as well, because it's not the done thing to mix with those awful outers.'

Lexi laughed.

Both of their life-loggers vibrated at the same time. 'Put that on hold,' Lexi said as she read the message. 'Looks like we've got another job.'

'Together. Someone on high must think we did all right as a team.'

'It's a high-security lab full of dead scientists in Shallow End.'

'Sounds gruesome,' Troy said. 'And obviously not as high security as they thought.'

Lexi stood up and brushed the soil away from her elbows. 'Charge your batteries some other time. This'll be good. It's the unit that handles all the science for The National Space Centre. Perhaps we'll get a ride into space. I've always fancied being an astronaut.'

The real science behind the story

The crimes in all of *The Outer Reaches* books are inspired by genuine scientific issues and events. Here are a few details of the science that lies behind *Body Harvest*.

Two species

The presence on Earth of two human species is not fantasy. Tens of thousands of years ago, *Homo sapiens*, Neanderthals and Denisovans were all alive. There was even a bit of interbreeding going on.

Neanderthals and Denisovans became extinct and *Homo sapiens* (that's us) continued. In *The Outer Reaches,* I imagine that one of the other humanoid races did not die out and evolved into outers. *Homo sapiens* became majors.

The outers' diet

While I have imagined a second human race called outers, I have not made up their diet. All of their meals are genuine bug-based food from around the world. Eating insects and arachnids is called entomophagy. It is much better for the Earth's resources to eat insects instead of meat. It takes 10 kg of feed to produce 1 kg of beef but only 1.7 kg of feed to make 1 kg of edible crickets. Weight-for-weight, insect farming releases only 1 per cent of the greenhouse gases emitted by raising sheep and cows and it uses far less water.

Trade in body parts

There is an illegal trade in body parts. It is driven by a shortage of organs donated on death. Gangs harvest organs from vulnerable and desperate people, and sometimes from executed prisoners and murder victims. In 2012, the World Health Organisation estimated that 10,000 black-market operations involving bought human organs happen every year, earning fortunes for the traffickers and surgeons.

Malcolm Rose is an established, award-winning author, noted for his gripping crime/thriller stories – all with a solid scientific basis.

Before becoming a full-time writer, Malcolm was a university lecturer and researcher in chemistry.

He says that chemistry and writing are not so different. *'In one life, I mix chemicals, stew them for a while and observe the reaction. In the other, I mix characters, stir in a bit of conflict and, again, observe the outcome.'*